SOUT
SECRETS
Sins of the Past

RICK RICHARDSON
SANDRA DEE

Southern Secrets
Sins of the Past

v3.0 r1.1

Image of Timothy Meaher is courtesy of Erik Overbey Collection, The Doy Leale McCall Rare Book and Manuscript Library, University of South Alabama.

Image of Cudjo "Kazoola" Lewis is courtesy of Erik Overbey Collection, The Doy Leale McCall Rare Book and Manuscript Library, University of South Alabama.

Outskirts Press, Inc.
http://www.outskirtspress.com

ISBN Paperback: 978-1-4327-9215-2
ISBN Hardback: 978-1-4327-9216-9

PRINTED IN THE UNITED STATES OF AMERICA

To my ancestors who made that final journey,
and sought peace and solace in America.
Areba & Ossa and Annie Keeby

ACKNOWLEDGMENTS

I would like to thank my family, especially my wife and parents for supporting me. A special thanks to Rachael, Julian, and Debbie, and Helen, Diane, and Lary for inspiring me.

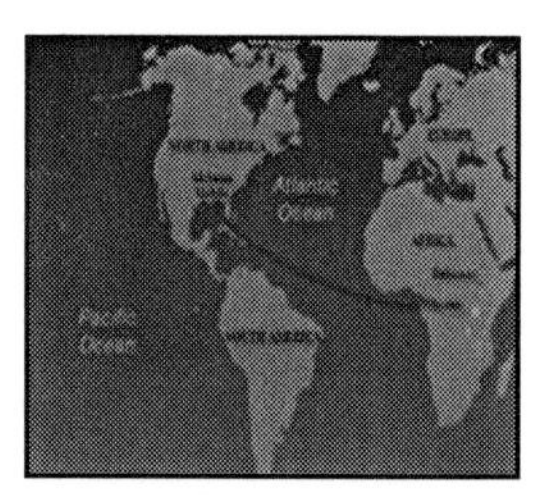

The voyage of the *Clotilda* from Mobile, Alabama, to Whydah, Africa, in 1859.

FOREWORD

The first slave ship came to America in 1619. It was a Dutch warship from the West Indies called the *White Lion*. It docked in Jamestown, Virginia, with twenty Africans onboard. Their arrival was a part of the trans-Atlantic slave trade, which took place from 1619 until 1808.

The United States Congress banned the importation of slaves from Africa on March 2, 1807, and the law took effect on January 1, 1808. The law stipulated that violators were to be fined $800 for knowingly buying illegally imported slaves and fined $20,000 or imprisoned for importing slaves. The fates of the illegally imported slaves were left up to the state legislatures. The new law came about because of anti-Black sentiment, but it was poorly enforced.

Although the government declared the importation of Africans for slave labor illegal in 1808, this by no means outlawed the domestic slave trade. Plantation owners and slave merchants were still able to trade slaves for other slaves and goods within the continental United States borders. With the growth of staple crops in the 1850s, the demand for slaves began to skyrocket, and there was a concerted effort among some in the slave-owning community to secretly import Africans as slaves.

Mobile, Alabama, known as "Cotton City," holds the unenviable distinction of being the port of entry for the last slaves kidnapped and brought into the United States, on a ship called the *Clotilda*.

As this story of those unwilling passengers shows, African-American history, American history, and African history are intertwined with the passion and persistence of the human spirit.

CHAPTER ONE
Mobile, Alabama 1965

Ten-year-old Ricky stared at the white 1964 Buick LeSabre as it slowly crept down the loose gravel road toward him. He walked behind a noisy push lawn mower cutting his family's large lawn and continued to stare at the beautiful car, proud that his daddy, Cliff, was behind the wheel. After cutting one last row of high grass, he quickly pushed the mower into the shed on the side of the old, gray Southern-style home he shared with his father, mother, and four siblings. As he walked out of the shed the glistening white Buick came to a stop in front of the house.

Ricky sprinted to the open driver's side window as dust settled. "Daddy, are we still going fishing?"

"Slow down, Ricky," Cliff said with a smile. "Can't you let your daddy out of the car first?"

Ricky backed away from the door and waited impatiently. Cliff took his time easing his tall, slender frame out of the car. He closed the door behind himself and turned to his son. "Now," he said. "Did you finish your chores?"

"Every one of them, Daddy."

"Well, I guess since it's a nice day and you finished your chores, I will take you fishing over at the bay," Cliff said, his smile bright against his smooth dark skin.

"Oh yes! That's where we catch those big mouth trout?" asked Ricky.

"Yep, just hurry and eat your breakfast," Cliff answered. "We want to get them early."

After breakfast Cliff and Ricky loaded up the car with fishing poles, a tackle box, and two sack lunches. Ricky twirled playfully, waving his arms in the warm summer breeze filled with the scent of cherry blossoms.

"You comin', son?" Cliff asked. Ricky stopped his spinning and jumped into the car. Thirty minutes later he could hear waves crashing against the rocks at the water's edge, forcing foam onto the shore.

Cliff parked near the shore in the gravel between two large boulders. Ricky jumped out of the car before Cliff could turn off the ignition. They grabbed their fishing gear and lunch and strolled along the shoreline. They stepped over rocks and overgrown weeds, listening to the sound of reeds thumping against the rocks. Soon they found a good spot and quietly set down their things, careful not to scare the fish away. Ricky baited his hook and cast his line. Before his father could even cast his line, Ricky caught a palm-sized blue gill.

"You got one already?" Cliff asked.

"Yeah, but it's too small," Ricky sighed. He unhooked the fish and threw it back into the bay. Ricky baited his line once more.

"Cast your line near that old piece of shipwreck," Cliff said. "That's where you caught that big mouth trout last time we were here."

Ricky looked to where his father pointed. "Is that part

of the ship sticking out of the water, Daddy?"

"That is the ship's keel and spine. See those pieces of split wood and rusted steel?" Ricky nodded. "They're from the front end of the ship. The wreck has been there for a very long time."

"Wow, I'm going to pitch my line right next to that old piece of wood with a hole in it," Ricky said. He raised the pole over his shoulder and cast his line. He settled himself on a large boulder to wait for his big catch. His father cast his line into the bay close to Ricky's line and sat next to Ricky with anticipation.

"You said that those pieces were from a shipwreck, Daddy?" Ricky inquired. "Where did the ship come from?"

Cliff stared at those bits of wood and steel for a long moment before he answered his son. "When I was about your age, my grandfather, your great-grandfather, Papa, told me that those were pieces from the last illegal slave ship to come to America. The ship was called the *Clotilda*."

"Do you mean real slaves, Daddy?"

"Let's put down the poles," he said. They stuck their fishing poles between two big rocks just in case a fish snagged the bait. "What I'm about to tell you is not in any history book," he began. "Your great-granddad, Papa, was married to Minnie, your great-grandmother who died before you were born. She was the daughter of Areba your great-great-grandmother, who came from Africa on that ship," Cliff said.

Ricky looked at the pieces of ship and then at his dad with amazement. "My great-grandma's mama was a real slave? And she came here on that ship?"

Cliff nodded. "In 1859 slavery was still going on, but at that point in time, the slave trade itself had been abolished and was illegal," he began. "But that didn't matter to some of the white men." Dark clouds rolled in over the bay. "The story is that one of these men made a bet that he could go to Africa and bring back a ship full of slaves, which he did. The *Clotilda* was the last slave ship to come to the United States, and that piece of junk right over there, is all that's left of her. She's over one hundred years old."

A flash of lightning lit the sky, and rain began to pour down on them. Ricky and his father grabbed their fishing gear and ran to the car, without any fish to bring home.

Once in the car, Ricky had so many questions that one after the other rolled from his mouth. "Dad, do we know what happen to all of those people on the ship? Were they separated from their families in Africa? I would hate to be separated from you, Mama, and my sisters and brothers. What happened when they got here?" Ricky got on his knees in the front seat and turned to look out the back window. He could see the remains of the ship grow smaller and smaller as they drove away. Ricky stared at the shipwreck until he couldn't see it anymore. He turned back around in his seat. When he spoke again, his voice was serious and sad. "Daddy, how did that ship get wrecked in the bay? Did the people on it drown?" Ricky stared at his father, waiting for answers.

"Oh boy, I cannot answer all of those questions, Ricky. Papa would be the best person to ask, but we really shouldn't bother him about slavery questions," Cliff replied.

"Why not, Daddy?"

"Let's just say that he is real sensitive about that topic.

He doesn't like to talk about it."

This piqued Ricky's interest even more. "Daddy, would you get mad at me if I asked him anyway?"

"Of course not, son," Cliff said. "But you have to respect his feelings. Tell you what. Go ahead and ask Papa about the ship, and if he doesn't want to talk about it, just stop asking. Agreed?"

"Agreed. I'm going to ask him tomorrow," Ricky said. Within a few minutes the constant tapping of the rain on the hood and smooth drive along the highway put Ricky into a somber sleep for the rest of the drive home.

That night, though, Ricky had trouble falling asleep. He lay on his back staring at the ceiling with his hands folded behind his head thinking about the *Clotilda* and the people on it, especially his great-great-grandmother, Areba. Everything would have been different if she hadn't come to America on that ship.

Ricky was so glad Papa was still around to talk to. He loved to listen to Papa preach at church on Sundays and tell folktales on Mondays and the rest of the week. In fact, everybody loved to listen to him talk. He looked like someone people should pay attention to, tall, broad shouldered, and clean cut in his Sunday best. But Papa didn't just preach and tell stories. He also worked hard at the fertilizer factory, and he could fix just about anything. Ricky remembered his first wagon. Papa had made it from old scraps of wood, and Ricky had wanted to take it everywhere. Ricky's eyes closed and he turned onto his left side, curled into a fetal position, and dreamed of his family.

Ricky woke early the next morning to the smell of bacon and fresh biscuits. Immediately, his thoughts went to the *Clotilda*. He couldn't wait to ask Papa about it. He quickly washed, dressed, and ran to the kitchen for breakfast.

"Morning, Mama," he said, grabbing a plate. Ricky loaded his plate with food, a strip of bacon halfway to his mouth before he sat down.

"Slow down, boy!" Mama ordered.

"I can't, Mama. I need to hurry so I can catch Papa before church."

"Why are you going over there?"

"Daddy showed me a slave ship right down there where we fish," Ricky answered around a mouthful of biscuit. "He said that Papa knows all about it, and I want to hear what happened to the people who came from Africa." He grabbed his plate, scraped the scraps into the trash, rinsed the plate, and ran through the flimsy screen door. "I'll be back before church, Mama," he called.

He jumped onto his blue stingray bike and pedaled as fast as he could. The bike couldn't go fast enough for Ricky, even though Papa's house was just half a mile down the road. Finally he turned into the driveway and came to a stop. He parked his bike next to the front porch, then bolted up the steps and flung open the screen door.

"Papa!" he called. There was no reply. He went to the kitchen. Out the window he could see Papa in the distance, walking through his garden in the back field.

Ricky went out to meet Papa, waving and calling to him. Papa walked toward the house, wiping the sweat from the back of his neck with his handkerchief.

"Hey boy, what's going on?" Papa asked as Ricky ran up to him. Papa grabbed a few figs from a nearby fig tree. He walked over to the water pump and pushed the handle downward three times with his old weathered hands, still strong. Water rushed out onto the figs.

"Daddy was telling me about that shipwreck in the bay, the *Clotilda*," Ricky began excitedly. "He said that you knew more about it than anybody else in the family, so I came by to hear about it. So tell me, Papa, what do you know about that ship?" A look came over Papa's face that Ricky had never seen before.

"Don't *ever* ask me about that ship again, boy!"

Ricky froze. He'd never heard Papa yell before.

Papa rubbed a hand over his face. "I'm sorry, Ricky," he said quietly. "I shouldn't have raised my voice like that." He put his arm around Ricky and handed him a fig. Ricky took the fig, still staring at Papa, and slowly put it into his mouth. They both sat, chewing on the figs. Papa looked at Ricky with curiosity. "That's not a topic I want to discuss, grandson," he said finally. "Why do you want to know about that ship?"

"Daddy took me fishing yesterday, and I saw what Daddy called the keel and the spine sticking out of the water right next to where we were throwing our lines. Daddy said that you would know all about the people on the ship. Won't you tell me what happened to them, Papa?" Ricky asked cautiously.

Papa leaned back thoughtfully. "Do you know old man Scott down the road?"

"Yeah," Ricky said. "He seems pretty mean to all of the

Black kids."

"Well, his dad owned my dad, and old man Scott has always hated Blacks. He treats every one of us hateful." Papa looked out over the fields. "It's a reminder I have every single day about how my father was treated by Whites. Every time I see him I remember what my papa went through. He had fifty whip scars across his back, thick and raised, and it made me want to kill someone."

"Did you kill anyone, Papa?" Ricky asked, his voice small.

"No Ricky, I never did," Papa said, looking down at his grandson. "I suppose that is why the good Lord wanted me to become a preacher, so I wouldn't kill." Papa stood up. "I have to get ready for church shortly, and you need to get home and get ready for church, too." They walked toward the house. "You also start school tomorrow and need to get ready for your first day back after the summer. Tell you what Ricky, check to see what you can find out at school this week, do good in school, and I will consider telling you about the *Clotilda* and all of the southern secrets next Saturday. Is that a deal?"

"It's a deal, Papa!" Ricky replied with excitement.

Papa reached in his pocket and pulled out a one-dollar bill and handed it to Ricky.

"Wow, thank you, Papa," Ricky said, squeezing Papa's middle in a tight hug. He ran over to his bike, hopped on, and pedaled for home.

The next morning Ricky got dressed, ate his breakfast, and arrived at school one hour early, eager to find what he could on the *Clotilda*. He searched throughout the library and was disappointed because there was so little information.

The rest of the day he sat in class daydreaming about the ship and the little he knew about it. At the end of the day, Ricky's teacher, Ms. Jones, gave the class an assignment to write a paper about Mobile. It was the first thing Ricky had heard all day. He knew that he would write about the *Clotilda*. Ricky raised his hand.

"Yes, Ricky?" Ms. Jones asked.

"Have you ever heard of the *Clotilda*?"

"Well, yes I have," Ms. Jones said, a bit surprised. "It was the last illegal slave ship to come to America, but I'm afraid that I do not know much more than that. I'm sorry, Ricky. But perhaps you can do your report on the topic and teach all of us more about the *Clotilda*?" Ms. Jones smiled at him.

Ricky's mouth dropped. He was very disappointed that his teacher could not offer more information. After all, she was supposed to be a historian, the smartest person around. The bell rang and the students eagerly began leaving class.

"Ricky!" Ms. Jones said. He paused in the doorway. "I look forward to reading your paper." Ricky gave a small smile and left.

After school on Tuesday and Wednesday, Ricky played with children in the neighborhood. On Thursday, he shopped with his mother, and on Friday, he completed all of his chores. When he came into contact with residents of Mobile, he took the opportunity to ask them questions about the *Clotilda*. Unfortunately, no one knew much more than he already knew.

The sun shined brightly on Ricky's face at 6:20 A.M. His eyes flew open when he realized it was Saturday morning! He hurried to wash himself and dress. He ran into his parents' bedroom to kiss them good-bye and tell them that he was headed to Papa's house. He grabbed his book-bag and rode his blue stingray to Papa's in less than eight minutes that morning.

"Hey boy," Papa said when Ricky appeared at his door. "You're up early today. How was your first week of school?"

"Fine Papa, but my teacher doesn't know anything."

"Well, keep going anyway. I'm sure you will learn something over time. Have you had breakfast yet?"

"No Papa, I was too excited to see you."

"Well then, grab some of the breakfast I cooked and come on out to the yard with your food. I will have a chair waiting for you next to the barbecue pit and the pecan tree," Papa said smiling.

Ricky grabbed heaping spoonfuls of hot grits, bacon, eggs, and two pieces of toast with apple butter before heading outside.

"My, my, what an appetite! That should hold you awhile," Papa observed.

Ricky began piling food into his mouth. "Papa, our teacher asked us to write about Mobile. I want my report to be the best, and I think that you can help me if you tell me about the *Clotilda*. I tried to find out what I could, like you told me to, but no one seems to know about it."

"Well, in that case, let me tell you what I know," Papa began.

"Wait a minute, Papa." Ricky put his plate on the ground and rummaged through his book-bag. He pulled out a notebook and pencil, took up his plate, and balanced everything on his lap. With a mouthful of food, Ricky mumbled, "I have to take notes for my report."

"Well, okay, I guess you know what you're doin'," Papa assented.

Ricky leaned forward expectantly, pencil poised over the open notebook.

"It all started with my wife Minnie's family," Papa began. "Her mama was a very strong African woman named Areba. She was kidnapped by a warring tribe and sold to the White men. In 1859, Mobile was called 'Cotton City' because so much cotton was produced here." Papa looked at Ricky. "You know that plantation owners used slaves to grow and pick the cotton, don't you?"

Still chewing his food, Ricky nodded.

"Well, by 1859 bringing Africans over here to be slaves was illegal. But the plantation owners still wanted more slaves because they were growing so much cotton. So men would still take ships across the Atlantic to buy slaves, even though there were man-of-war ships, the authorities from Europe and America, out there waiting to catch them."

"And the *Clotilda* was the last illegal slave ship to come to America! Right, Papa?" Ricky interjected.

"Yes," Papa agreed. "I'm sure you know Mobile is a port city, and slave ships, legal and illegal, used to dock here. But it wasn't only slave ships. All kinds of ships came here, and travelers and businessmen were constantly passing through. One such person to pass through Mobile was Captain Timothy Meaher."

CHAPTER TWO
February 1859

Timothy Meaher lit a pipe and let the match fall into the swells of water that splashed against the steamboat moving along the Mississippi. He made his way across the steamboat deck toward Captain Robert Taney.

"Afternoon, Captain Taney," Meaher muttered.

"Afternoon, Captain Meaher."

"So how's business?"

Folding his newspaper, Taney stood. "Business is booming!" he said sarcastically. "To be honest, we need more slaves. The crops are growing so fast they will end up going bad if we don't get more help soon."

"Things can't be that bad," Meaher said.

"That's easy for you to say, sir. You have twenty of them working your fields. Got any to spare?"

"Not at all. You don't know what I went through to get the ones I have," Meaher said smiling. He turned toward the roar of laughter and loud words of drunken men inside the steamboat bar. "Hey." Meaher gestured to Captain Taney. "Let me buy you a drink?"

"Don't you own this ship and everything in it?" asked Taney.

"Sure do," he allowed. "But I make sure profits are made at every opportunity, even if I'm supporting myself. A rich man doesn't take advantage of small things, so I buy my own drinks." Meaher winked at Taney.

They shuffled down six plank steps and swung open the door to the bar. The sound of the commotion inside made Meaher's ears ring. As he walked over to the bar, he shook hands with many familiar locals.

One of those familiar faces was the bartender who yelled to Meaher, "Hey, Captain Meaher, what's it gonna be?"

"Give me a whiskey, and give them whatever they're drinking," Meaher said, pointing to the table closest to the bar where his lifelong friend Captain William Foster sat talking to a stranger. Meaher and Taney grabbed stools from the bar and dragged their seats to Captain Foster's table.

Captain Foster greeted the men and grabbed Meaher's shoulder, directing his attention to the man at his table. "May I introduce my friend John Taylor, a businessman from New York."

Taylor shook Meaher's hand and thanked him for the drink. "I really don't need it. My woman is gonna have a fit." Taylor paused then said, "Then again, I just might get lucky!" The men broke out in laughter.

"Speaking of luck," Foster said, "Mr. Taylor and I were just talking about how well crops are growing in these parts."

"I never imagined when I bought the old Fenton Plantation that crops would grow as well as they are," John Taylor added.

"So what brought you to Mobile, Mr. Taylor?" Meaher asked. The others leaned in to hear Taylor's response.

"Well, New York's economy has slowed tremendously. The banks and businesses are hurting pretty bad right now. I wanted to take my wealth to a place where I could build on it, not lose it. What better place than the cotton city, Mobile? So I purchased my own land right in the middle of it all, and here I am," Taylor said proudly.

"So how about you, Captain Timothy Meaher? You seem to be the man to know. What's your business, other than owning this wonderful steam boat?" Taylor asked.

Foster stood with a drink in one hand and put his other around Meaher's shoulders. "This man has several businesses. He is a very successful shipbuilder who owns a lumber mill, a cotton plantation, and three steamships, which he uses to transport large barrels of cotton up the Mississippi."

"Is all that true, Captain?" Taylor asked.

Before Meaher could answer, Foster continued. "Two of his steamships travel fifty-three miles one way from Mobile, Alabama to Biloxi, Mississippi, with various stops in small towns in between the two states. He delivers cotton from Alabama and Mississippi to ports where it's sold to various dressmakers and textile markets."

Taney broke in. "Let me add that Meaher's third steamship is for taxying mostly rich landowners from North to South."

"Well, Meaher," Taylor observed, "Your friends sure do know how to make you sound impressive."

"And we're not done," Taney continued.

"That's enough," said Meaher, holding up his hand.

Taney lowered his voice and leaned in closer. "Captain Meaher here also uses his boats to smuggle slaves from Mississippi to Alabama."

"How do you know about that, Taney?" Meaher asked sharply.

"I make it my business to know about everyone else's business, sir. I'm always looking for a way to build on my own fortune," Taney replied with a smile. He picked up a paper lying on the table. "Look at this, 'Cotton City Booming'," he said reading the headline aloud.

"Hell!" Meaher said. "Leo down the road told me that it looks like he's going to make twice as much as he did last year 'cause those cotton crops are growing so good."

"I heard it was because of those niggers from Africa they smuggled up there in Mississippi? Those slaves really put out the work," Foster replied. "The cotton's growing for me too. But I just ain't got enough niggers to help out. If I had about thirty more of them, I could triple my profits. I wish I could smuggle me some niggers."

"Well, it looks like we're just going to have to get some!" Meaher yelled, slightly drunk.

John Taylor looked around the room hoping no one had heard the man's outburst. He leaned forward, turned to Meaher, and half-whispered, "You know smuggling niggers is outlawed. White folks are being hanged for that."

A gentleman nearby had heard Meaher, and he made his way to their table and invited himself into the conversation. "Yeah, hanging is supposed to scare off smugglers, and protect those of us who are trying to make an honest living!"

All of the men turned toward the newcomer. Taylor stood to greet him. "Hello, Reed. What are you doing here?"

"Hello, John Taylor. I thought that was you."

"Gentlemen, this is Paul Reed from New York." Everyone shook hands and Reed pulled a chair up to their table. "Now if I were the law," he said, "all you would be headed to the jailhouse. I overhead you say that you wanted to get yourselves some more slaves, but you are risking being hanged if caught." Taylor nodded in agreement.

"Nonsense," Meaher answered. "Nobody will be hanged and the law doesn't scare anybody."

"Congress banned the importation of slaves from Africa, and the British Navy and American man-of-war ships are out in those waters waiting for people just like you," Reed said.

Meaher snorted and sipped his drink.

"Come on, Meaher," Reed continued, determined. "For bringing them over here you will be hanged and anyone who knowingly buys illegally imported slaves will be fined eight hundred dollars. And just for equipping a slave ship, the fine is up to twenty thousand or imprisonment."

"No one can bring in slaves any more, not even you, Meaher," Taylor added.

Suddenly, Meaher jumped up from his chair and announced, "It is very feasible. In fact, I bet each of you fifty thousand dollars that it can be done. I bet you that within four months we can bring some African niggers into Mobile Bay right under the officers' noses."

Startled, Reed and Taylor looked at each other and then stared at Meaher, not sure what to make of his drunken bet.

Captain Taney, meanwhile, sat by with a big smile on his face thinking about the profits he could make if he used his connections with law enforcement to make the bet work in Meaher's favor.

Taylor persisted in his doubt. "Meaher, even if you made it to Africa, you'd be caught upon your return with a ship full of slaves."

Taney decided to prod the gentlemen. "You know those New York gentlemen don't have the balls to take such a bet." Everyone but Reed and Taylor burst into loud laughter.

Taney waited for the New Yorkers to take on the bet. The gentlemen whispered to one another and then Taylor reached across the table, grabbed Meaher's hand, and shook it. "You got a bet." Reed did the same. "I look forward to winning fifty thousand from you after you're caught," Taylor added.

Meaher grinned. "We'll just wait and see who's out fifty grand."

Taylor and Reed stood. "We will see you gentlemen when you return and we will be waiting for our money," said Taylor. "If you are arrested, make sure to send someone with our money." They both laughed and walked away from the table.

Meaher sobered a bit, realizing that he'd just made a bet that would either make him $100,000 richer or poorer. Foster and Taney looked at him in silence.

"Well, I guess we're going to have to make this work," Meaher said. "I need two seamen with great sea legs. The two I am thinking of are the best in Mobile. Foster, you are the best sailor in the South. I need you to captain the ship.

Taney, I know all about your vast sailing history and will need you as first mate." Before they could reply, Meaher rushed on. "You won't have to put up any money in the bet and you will be compensated very well, with money and slaves. How does that sound?"

Foster and Taney looked at one another for a moment then both held out their hands for Meaher to shake.

Meaher stood as the boat slowed. "We're just about to dock in Mobile. Stick around after everyone leaves and we'll make plans."

"Okay," said Foster.

"Gladly." Taney nodded.

"Good. We will need a few weeks to get ready, plus two months each way. My estimate is that we should arrive in late July, somewhere around the twenty-ninth," Meaher announced to the group. He grabbed a bottle of scotch and poured three shots. The men walked over to the bar where Taylor and Reed were still sitting. They held their glasses up high and toasted the event. "Here's to good sailing and lots of money," Meaher proclaimed.

"Or bad sailing and lots of money," shouted Taylor with a nod to Reed.

The boat docked in Mobile Bay and shortly after finishing the round of drinks, Reed and Taylor left. Meaher, Foster, and Taney huddled together at the end of the bar. They agreed to meet the next evening at the docks to work out the details of the voyage and to take a look at the ship that was to sail.

CHAPTER THREE

Papa grew tired of sitting in the lawn chair and stood to stretch. He glanced at Ricky, who seemed spellbound by the story.

"Why did you stop, Papa?"

"I'm thirsty. How about you, boy?"

"Yep. What do have to drink?"

"Pick up your plate and toss those scraps into the garbage on the side of the house, then come in and wash your plate. I will meet you in the kitchen."

Ricky tossed his scraps as he was told and climbed up the porch steps. He saw old man Scott looking back at him from the other side of the hedges. He stared at Ricky without saying a word. Ricky also kept quiet and went inside to meet Papa.

In the kitchen, Papa laid out two glasses, some ice, a large spoon, and a package of sugar next to a pitcher of Kool-Aid. "Ricky, stand on that footstool and stir that sugar into the pitcher of grape Kool-Aid. Not too much of that sweet stuff in that Kool-Aid, boy. I got 'sugar,' you know."

Ricky climbed up and carefully poured two glasses of Kool-Aid under Papa's watchful eye. Papa led Ricky to the kitchen table and they sat down to their drinks. When Papa's glass was empty, Ricky opened his notebook and picked up his pencil. "Now are you ready to tell me some more?"

"Yes, Ricky."

After leaving Meaher's steamboat, Foster returned to his plantation. He sat in his bedroom and fell asleep thinking about the trip to Africa. He woke from an alarming dream and found himself sweaty and his heart racing.

Downstairs in his study, he poured himself a shot of whiskey and sat in his favorite chair, still feeling upset about the dream.

Nia, a beautiful thirteen-year-old slave girl with cocoa brown skin, walked past the study and noticed Foster's troubled demeanor. She stopped in the doorway. "Is there anything I can do for you, Mister Foster?" she asked quietly.

Foster looked at the slave girl for a moment. He realized that he needed her company. "Come in, Nia. I'm having trouble sleeping and I would like to tell you about a bad dream I had tonight."

Nia walked into the room and stood next Foster. As always, he felt calmer now that Nia was near.

"The dream starts with the seas," he told her. "They are dark, stormy and fierce, almost like a gateway to hell. The shipmates are screaming. Everyone on board is screaming. As the ship is tussled, men are dying and waves overtake the ship. I see death—everywhere around me. "Foster looked at Nia, searching her face. Her dark eyes were so warm and beautiful that Foster felt lost in them and almost forgot what he was saying. He caught himself. "What is it, Nia, what does this dream mean? You have always been able to tell me about my dreams. I don't know how you do it, but I need your help once again."

Nia walked over to a mirror hanging on the wall, reached inside of her apron and closed her fingers around two stones, rubbing them quietly together and searching her heart for the meaning of his dream. She turned back to him she said, "The dream is a strong sign of things to come. There will be a journey of evil and you, Mister Foster, are involved." She stepped closer to him, looking into his eyes. "You should not make this journey, sir. It will only bring pain for many."

Foster gazed at her, unsure. "You know, you have never shared with me how you can do that, Nia. How do you interpret dreams?"

"It is a gift that my sister and I share, but her gift is more powerful than mine," she replied.

"I never knew you had a sister, Nia," Foster said as he walked over to the window and stared into blackness. "Why do you and your sister have such a special gift?"

"I don't know, sir," Nia responded. "Perhaps it is a gift from the heavens, similar to our gift of knowing different languages. My mother was taught many languages from religious foreigners and she taught us everything she learned. My sister and I have always been kissed with special blessings."

He turned and looked at her. "You are a very special

person, Nia. You are very special to me in many ways, and I always protect my interest. You are my good luck charm and you will always be by my side. In fact, you were correct about the dream. I will soon be going on a journey. To Africa, and you will be coming with me."

Nia was shocked at his words. She had not seen Africa since she was taken by White men several years ago.

At that moment she realized just how much she missed her family and felt a sudden excitement. Her heart pumped heavily and she suppressed her joy to keep Foster from knowing how much she wanted to be back on African soil.

"But now that you have mentioned tragedy, I am very apprehensive about going," Foster said. "Do you think that the ship will be lost at sea?"

"Oh no, sir, I must have said it wrong. I meant that the weather would be a little rough, but you will make it through," Nia responded.

"Well then, that sounds much better."

"When will we be traveling, sir?" Nia asked.

"Within two to three weeks."

"Very well, sir."

"Thank you, Nia. You may go."

Nia nodded and left the room. Pausing in the hallway, she pulled two stones from her apron. She smiled, thinking of Africa. Perhaps when she went to Africa, she could learn what happened to her family.

For now, she reconciled that she was a house slave for Foster. Each day she cleaned, cooked, and served meals. Sometimes she helped cook for the whole plantation. Even though the work was hard, Nia knew she was fortunate.

She knew she lived better than Foster's other slaves, up in her large attic room he'd made especially perfect for her.

Her thoughts were interrupted by a heavy knock on the front door and Nia promptly went to answer it.

"Hello, gal. I'm Captain Taney here on business to see Captain Foster," announced the man on the doorstep. "Is he home?"

"Yes, sir. I will take you to him. May I take your coat and hat, sir?" Nia ushered Taney into the large home and took his things before leading him to the study. "Sir, Captain Taney is here," Nia announced softly.

Captain Foster rose and the two men shook hands. Foster looked at Nia and nodded once. She remained standing nearby. Foster turned to Taney. "So what brings you here, Taney? I thought we agreed to meet tomorrow."

Taney looked at the slave woman with a scowl and back at Foster, waiting for him to dismiss her.

"Nia stays," Foster told him. "What can I do for you, Captain Taney?"

Taney frowned at the young woman. Foster was in dangerous territory. Slaves were not to be trusted, especially not young pretty ones like this girl. Taney realized Foster had asked him a question and tore his gaze away from her.

"Sir, I didn't want to talk about this in front of the others earlier, but I have some connections with law enforcement that can provide the protection we need for the journey. It is a sure way of getting"—he looked at Nia and chose his words carefully—"our cargo into the United States and to ensure that we will win that bet. But in order for me to make that happen, I will need a little something extra."

Foster raised his eyebrows and crossed the room to look out the tall window into the darkness. Finally, he turned to Taney. "Just what are you asking for and what guarantee do we have?"

"The price is a fraction of what you stand to gain from the success of the trip. I will need ten thousand, half up front and the rest prior to our travels. As far as the guarantee, there are seamen on those U. S. Navy ships who will slow down the ship if it gives chase, assuring that they will never catch us."

"Guaranteed, huh?" Foster paused. "I am positive that Meaher will put up half up front for that guarantee.

"Nia, would you go get glasses of cold water for me and Mr. Taney, please."

"So what's that all about, Captain?" Taney asked when she was gone. "It's pretty unheard of for women, let alone slave women, to hang around during a business conversation," Taney said.

"Dear sir, what I do in my home is no business of yours." Foster returned to his place in front of the window. "Nia is different than the others. I trust her."

Taney frowned. "Don't be a fool, man!" Taney stopped talking when Nia entered the room with cold drinks.

"This better work just as you described, Taney, and I don't need any more of your advice."

"Oh, it will work, sir," Taney assured him. "I will see you tomorrow evening and we will discuss the plan with Meaher." Taney headed toward the door. Both Foster and Nia walked with Taney through the corridor to the front door and saw him out.

After Foster closed the door behind Taney, he turned

to Nia. "Something about that man just doesn't feel quite right," Foster said quietly. Nia looked at the floor and shook her head slowly.

"What is it, Nia?" Foster asked. "You feel it too, about Taney, don't you?"

Nia looked up. "Sir, I'm not sure if you will like what I have to say." He waited for her to speak. "Sir, your visitor isn't a good person and shouldn't be trusted."

"You may be right about Taney, Nia," Foster admitted. "I will keep my eye on him during our journey to Africa. Since you will be with me and will have some freedom on the ship, you must tell me at once if you see anything suspicious."

"Oh, I will sir," Nia responded.

"You may turn in for the night, Nia." Nia nodded and turned to go. "Wait!" Foster said. He took Nia's arm and gently opened the button at her neck. "I will see you shortly," Foster said. Nia held his gaze a moment then gently pulled away. Foster watched her climb the stairs until he could no longer see her.

Taney returned to his plantation and called his servant into the study to pour him a glass of whiskey on the rocks. "Dela," he called. There was no reply. "Dela," he called once again. Grumbling, he walked down the long hallway toward the kitchen. He heard Dela and another servant, Annie, chatting as they cleaned. He stood out of sight and listened to the two women gossiping.

"Ya know, I heard dey headed back over there to get some mo' Negroes," said Dela.

"Na girl, you must be kiddin'. How did you hear that?" Annie asked.

"Meaher's slave Buster was loadin' up supplies to take to the shipyard and he was talkin' out there about what Taney and dem Whites was gonna do. Dey goin' over ta Africa to get mo' slaves," Dela said.

"I bet you anything that Foster take his precious Nia wit him," said Annie, scrubbing harder at the pot in her hands.

"And I bet he don't even know she got dem shinin' rocks she be carrin' everywhere she go, thinkin' they got super powers," Dela added, shaking her head.

"She carries them with her everywhere?" Annie asked, raising her eyebrows. "You ever seen 'em? What do they look like? And what purpose do they serve for her to carry them?"

"Well, I saw dem once. Dey look like little pieces of glass. Dey say she can read dreams wit 'em, but I think that's just foolishness. Some African mumbo jumbo that has nothin' to do wit dem rocks. Her sister Areba carries rocks too, but she's still in Africa," Dela replied.

"How you know about all dis business?" asked Annie.

"The sisters, Areba and Nia, are from my village in Africa. I used ta fetch water in the same waterway with dem girls and dey mama. One day lots of chil'ren were playin' in the waterway and Areba told everybody to get out. After dey was out, a big poison snake zipped across the water. She seemed to see it before it ever showed." Dela's face became somber. "Then Nia and I were captured two days later by dem Whites, and they brought us here on the same ship." The two women were silent a moment.

Finally Dela joked, "I wish I could go back to Africa right now. I'd disappear and leave dees pots burnin' right where dey is." Annie grinned.

Suddenly, the kitchen door opened and they turned to see Taney standing in the doorway.

"Didn't you hear me, woman?" he demanded, looking at Dela. "Git in the study and fix my drink." Dela hurried to the study and poured bourbon midway in a glass. When she finished pouring, she brought the drink over to Taney.

"So, what was that I heard you saying about some shining rocks?" he asked.

"Oh nothing, sir," she lied. "I was just making stories." She held the glass out to him. He reached for the drink, but grabbed her wrist instead, holding it roughly and looking into her eyes.

"You know what will happen if I catch you lying to me, right?"

Dela held still. Taney tightened his grip. Finally she said, "Well sir, we was just talkin' 'bout Massa Foster's woman, Nia. She has some shinin' rocks that she's had since a young child, and people believe dem rocks give her some kind of powers over dreams. It's all foolish talking, sir. I was just telling Annie that Nia's sister Areba has some of those rocks too, but she's in Africa."

Taney let go of her wrist. He sipped his drink and looked at her doubtfully, but couldn't deny his curiosity. "Have you ever seen the rocks?" he asked.

"Yes, sir," Dela responded.

"And what do they look like?"

Dela shrugged and looked down. "Well, sir, dey look

like that ring you got there, but a whole lot bigger," she said, pointing at his finger.

Taney sat up straight in his chair. "Do you mean to tell me that Nia's rocks look like this?" he asked, pointing at the diamond in the middle of the gold on his ring.

"Yes, sir," Dela replied.

"How many shining rocks does Nia have?" asked Taney.

"Well, I only remember seeing her with two when we was little, and her sister had some too, but I don't know how many. I hear she always keeps them close—somewhere on her body," Dela said.

"Just how big are the rocks, Dela?" Taney asked carefully.

She took her middle finger and thumb and showed Taney a circle. "About the size of the pit of a peach, sir."

She watched Taney's eyes grow. She didn't understand why he was so excited about a peach pit, but she was afraid to ask any questions.

"That's all, Dela. You've been very helpful tonight." Taney looked away, already plotting in his mind. "Leave me," he directed. She left the room immediately.

All through the night Taney thought about how he could get his hands on Nia's "shining rocks," especially since she was always in Foster's presence.

CHAPTER FOUR

The next evening Meaher and Foster met at the docks to discuss the details of the trip. Taney had not yet arrived.

"Good evening, Foster," Meaher said.

Foster tipped his hat in reply and the two walked along the dock toward one of Meaher's ships.

"There she is!" Meaher said, gesturing to the ship just ahead. "That's the one you'll be taking."

Foster looked at the ship with a disappointed scowl. It was much smaller than he had imagined it would be and the ship wasn't in good condition, at least not for the high seas.

"The deck is weathered and the mast is, too. It is quite small, don't you think?" Foster said.

"Her size is sufficient, Foster," Meaher replied defensively.

"You know, my father actually sailed to Whydah, Africa a couple of times to get slaves and made it home safely both times. He was a great sailor and taught me how to avoid the British man-of-war ships and the American Navy. He used one of his own special ships and it never let him down. You might want to consider using that ship for the journey. It has both speed and the capability of carrying large cargo. She's on the other side of the docks if you would like to see her," Foster offered.

Meaher took his hands from his pockets and located his pipe and matches. Clenching the pipe between his teeth, he struck a match on the side of an iron pole beside him. He lit the pipe and tilted his head back, inhaling the smoke. He exhaled slowly and walked along his ship, looking her over from front to back. When he had finished he returned to Foster.

"My ship will do fine, thank you Foster," Meaher announced.

"That ship will get you out for one day at most and then the ocean will send you running back to Mobile," Foster replied, exasperated. "This is not a trip up and down the Mississippi River or Mobile Bay. These are treacherous waters where we may see fifty-foot waves. The ship must have no less than two masts and should be at least eighty-five feet long with a copper hull. I have to tell you Meaher, you had such a nice fleet, and I really thought you would have something better for this trip.

"My father's ship has proven that it can cut through the waves and outrun the naval ships that will be tracking us down. The ship is already outfitted as a merchant ship. You know it is imperative that the ship's true purpose not be discernible," Foster said sternly.

"Where is this ship?" Meaher asked reluctantly.

"We call her the *Clotilda*; she's on the other side of the docks."

"Well, I suppose I should see it, especially since it has a *proven* record to make the trip and outrun the Navy ships, but let's wait for Taney. He should be here any minute."

Moments later they could see Taney in the distance, approaching the dock's entrance.

"By the way, Taney stopped by last night," Foster said. "He says he has connections in the navy. In exchange for our safe return, he wants a little something extra."

"Taney is always looking for a way to make a quick dollar. You have to watch him, Foster. He's been known to be very sneaky when he's after something. I should have known he wanted something when he agreed to be the first mate so quickly. Do we believe he can do it?"

"I don't suppose he'd agree to be first mate if he couldn't protect the ship."

"How much does he want?" Meaher asked.

"He wants ten grand," Foster said. Seeing Meaher's eyes widen, Foster held up his hands. "I wouldn't know any other way to keep the law off our backs."

"You're right, but there's something about him that doesn't sit right with me."

Foster recalled his conversation with Nia from the night before. It seemed everyone had the same misgivings about the man.

Taney reached the waiting pair. "Hello, gentlemen," he said, reaching out to shake hands.

"Hello, Taney," both men replied.

"Foster was just telling me about a schooner that is much better suited than the one I planned to take," Meaher said.

"What's wrong with your ship?" asked Taney.

"The schooner Foster is referring to has already seen several successful voyages to Africa and Foster seemed to think my offering is lacking, both in size and strength," Meaher explained drily.

"Let me show you both the schooner now," said Foster.

The three men proceeded to walk toward the other side of the docks. Foster continued, "I was just telling Meaher that the ship has the speed we will need and is large enough for all of the slaves we'll carry."

"What's her name?" Taney asked.

"*Clotilda*," Foster responded. "And there she is." Foster pointed at the large well-built ship not more than one hundred yards away. "She's garnished with two masts, eighty-six feet long and twenty-three feet wide, with a copper hull."

"I am quite impressed, Foster," Meaher admitted. "I would like to take a look around if it's okay with you."

As they boarded the *Clotilda*, she rocked gently, and the sound of empty shackles against wood greeted the men. They walked past piles of lumber, large iron pots, and barrels of water and food.

Taney peered into the containers of beans, rice, corn, and bread. "Is this food for the well-behaved slaves?" he joked. Foster and Meaher ignored the comment and continued looking around.

Meaher turned to Foster. "The ship does seem to be equipped perfectly for the business at hand. The items currently onboard, are they included?"

"Of course. I will take these goods into account when I give you my fee," Foster replied with a smile.

"Will this be enough food for the journey?" Taney asked.

"We have several wagons bringing more supplies on the day of departure, and you will pick up more at some of the ports during your travels and once you arrive in Africa," Meaher said. "I'm going to look below. A lantern, if I may, Foster?" Foster nodded and fetched a lantern.

Meaher lit it and made his way below deck. In the dim light he could make out shelves covering both walls, stacked three high. The shelves were about six feet in length. Each shelf bore its own set of shackles. Meaher was impressed by the *Clotilda*'s design. He had seen many slave ships in his day.

Meaher returned to the top deck stood next to Foster. "Well Foster, if you really believe that she will outrun those navy ships, then I will take you up on the offer."

"Very well," Foster said, pleased and proud that Meaher admitted the *Clotilda* was superior to his own schooners.

"And Taney, Foster tells me it will take ten grand for the protection on the high seas," said Meaher.

"That's right. If you want a guarantee that you will bring the cargo back undetected, it will cost you."

"So be it!" said Meaher. "I will deliver half of the money and the supplies the morning of departure. Foster, you just have the crew ready. Taney, I don't expect that you'll have any problems getting the slaves in, but if anything goes wrong, you will repay the five grand that I am putting up. I will only pay with a guaranteed delivery," Meaher said.

Taney interjected defensively, "Don't worry, gentlemen, my part is covered. We will have the protection we need, and because I am so confident that things will go well, I agreed to pay anything owed."

Meaher nodded, satisfied. Foster paced the boards and planned aloud. "It will take us fourteen days to get the crew and get her ready and loaded. As soon as we finish here, I will begin rounding up the men for the voyage, and putting them in the bow of the ship."

"What do you mean, put them in the bow of the ship?" Taney inquired.

Meaher smirked. "Foster has a unique way of collecting the crewmen for his voyages. Suffice it to say we will be testing out our new shackles before departure." Meaher and Foster looked at one another and burst with laughter.

"So, what is this unique method of collecting the crew, Foster?" Taney asked, not wanting to be left out of the joke.

"Let's just say I'll be land fishing," Foster replied.

"Marlin," Meaher added with a nod. The two men roared again and Meaher held his stomach. When Foster caught his breath, he turned to Taney. "My method is rather simple. I convince wenches from the brothel to lure stupid, drunken boys and men to a predetermined area and then they are bush-wacked, drugged, and taken on board." Foster smiled. "There are some who will come willingly," he added. "They do it for the money and will ignore everything they see. They follow the same code of silence as the captain and first mate. What happens aboard a ship at sea, only the winds know."

"Whether they come willingly or not, what's important is that we get a strong crew, eh, Foster?" said Meaher.

"Too true," Foster said. He looked at Taney. "The death

rate among slave ship crews is almost as high as deaths amongst the slaves, even on the healthiest of voyages." Foster looked out over the water. "Quite frankly, I'm tired of the seas. I am weathered in my bones and intend for this to be my last journey." He turned back to the men. "I wouldn't be going on this one if I weren't in such need of more slaves myself."

"Then may your last voyage be a successful one," Meaher said. "I think that our job is done here, gentlemen. I will take stock of your current supplies and make a list of anything else you will need for the journey. Foster, go ahead and round up your men tonight. The bow is ready for them."

Meaher nodded to the men and took his leave. He knew that the risk of getting caught with slaves in tow was great. A Morgan slayer ship had been caught up the Mississippi Narre a month past. The authorities wouldn't take a bribe for that illegal voyage. Old Captain Gold went to trial and quietly disappeared. His slaves were conveniently sent to their buyers.

Even with Captain Gold on his mind, Meaher still believed he had a chance to make this last sail a profitable one and felt confident that all would go as planned.

That night Foster met his men at a bar. Each man had come dressed in dark clothing, a black scarf tied around the neck. As Foster began talking with the men, Taney appeared.

"I decided to join you. For the experience," Taney said. Foster gave Taney a slight smile. The men pulled their chairs in around a small table.

"Men, we have plenty of work to do tonight. The gold rush in California has left the South with too few men fit for life at sea," Foster said. "I need at least forty men for a journey to Africa. You should use whatever means necessary to get the sailors we need. As you might suspect, the most straightforward method to shanghai a man is to render him unconscious." Foster looked around the table. "As members of my crew, you will be compensated based on the number of slaves that make it to Mobile alive and well. As further payment for your services, Captain Meaher will make each of you sailors with regular wages on his state-to-state voyages."

"Yeah!" the crimps shouted, the thought of having honorable work making joy evident on their faces. Foster held up his hands, asking for quiet, and they all hunkered over beer and made their plan of attack.

After finishing their drinks, Foster, Taney, and the crimps set out to capture enough men to make up a crew.

What the other men did not know was that Foster had an understanding with tavern owners around the docks. Thanks to the tavern owners, Foster knew which sailors had particularly large liquor debts.

On the night of the capture, Foster prompted the tavern owners to demand immediate payment and tell the sailors that they would go to jail if they could not pay their debts.

Foster then approached the desperate sailors with a deal: he would pay off their debts, and in return, the sailors would be on his crew. Each of the men accepted the offer and signed a contract and was taken to the ship by a couple of the crimps.

Outside the Devil's Tavern Foster noticed a young free Black man strolling past. "Hey!" he shouted. "Are you a seaman?"

The young man turned around, surprised. "Me? No sir, well, I was a ship carpenter at one time. Why do ya ask?"

"Because you look very familiar," replied Foster. "What's your name?"

"My name's Billy. I don't think I knows you, but I been out at sea for five years. The seas made me so ill, I stopped that line of work. I never want to see the open seas again. In fact, ya couldn't pay me to go back out dere," Billy said with a slight smile. "Well, ya'll have a nice night," he added, turning to go on his way.

Before he'd gone three steps, a group of men with black scarves covering their faces surrounded him. Billy cried out when a sack was put over his head, and kicked as hard as he could as they whisked him away into the night.

A small, stocky man dressed in business attire was looking for his friends near the docks. Taney approached him, feeling a bit cocky. He tapped the man on the shoulder. "Excuse me, I would like to know, what is your experience with shipping?"

In a familiar Southern strain the man asked, "What is shipping?"

Taney gave a whistle and in a flash, some of Foster's men emerged from the dark. Their new catch was dragged through several streets amid shocked onlookers.

When twenty-two-year-old Billy awoke, his head was pounding. He opened his eyes slowly. There was dim light coming from above, and he guessed it must be morning. Somehow he'd ended up deep within the bowels of what looked like a ship, and he almost gagged from the strong stench of mold and tar. He rolled onto his right side and pushed himself into a sitting position. He was sitting on a hard, flat surface, just long enough and wide enough for him to sleep on. When he stood up, a flash of pain shot through his head, and he put a hand to his forehead as he took in his surroundings. He noticed stairs and his first inclination was to bolt for them. Just then he looked across the room and saw a small, stocky White man in the darkness.

Billy became frightened. "Help!" he yelled loudly, grabbing his head from the pain he felt.

"Stop yelling!" the man said. "No one will come. We're alone."

"Where're we at?" Billy asked.

"On a ship, obviously," the man answered drily.

Billy sat back down on a nearby cot. "How long you been here?" he asked.

"Those bastards put me in this hole last night," he replied.

"Me too. I'm Billy. Billy Hansen, carpenter."

"I am Thomas Fitzpatrick, a businessman. I don't think they know how important I am."

"I don't know 'bout you, but I'ma look around for a way out here," Billy said. He stood up and felt his way along the rounded side of the ship. He noticed a small area without any cargo and moved into it. A row of spikes had been pounded into boards above his head. Curious, Billy moved closer. He froze in his tracks. From each spike hung a pair of leg irons. Each beam was outfitted with the same hardware.

"Why would a ship need hundreds of leg irons?" Billy wondered aloud. Then it hit him, "This is not a common merchant ship; it is a slave ship! Oh my God! What's goin on here? Is somebody tryin to make me a slave?" Billy yelled, but Thomas did not respond for he refused to believe what he had just heard.

That night the crimps met at the Devil's Tavern to have drinks and relive the excitement. As they drank and laughed, one crimp named Joseph noticed a man sitting close by, bragging loudly about his skill as a cook and naming all of the dishes he had prepared.

Joseph nudged a few other crimps to get their attention and nodded toward the braggart. The tall, slender man called himself Chef James. Just then he was rhapsodizing about his beef stew. The crimps thought that the chef would be a perfect candidate for the ship's cook. Joseph offered Chef James a drink—and asked the bartender to double the alcohol.

The crimps invited themselves into the chef's conversation, and continuously asked questions about food, keeping the drinks flowing. When Chef James was drunk enough, the crimps offered to take him home. Chef James agreed, nearly falling off his barstool. As soon as the crimps accompanied him outside, they bound and gagged him and took him to the ship.

Billy and Thomas looked when the hatch door opened above them. They walked right under the hatch and saw two sailors lowering an unconscious man down with a rope, followed by two containers of water and bread.

They looked up at the sailors and Fitzpatrick began yelling. "Let us out of here, you bastards!" The hatch closed and their eyes adjusted to the darkness once again. Both men grabbed a cup of water and a piece of bread.

Billy sat down to eat. Thomas set his rations aside and untied the man who had been thrown into the hull. The man came to and stared at Thomas.

"Where am I? Who are you and what am I doing here?" he asked.

"We are on a ship and someone has kidnapped all of us," Thomas told him.

"What!" the man said, looking around in disbelief.

"What is your name?" Thomas asked.

"James Johnson, better known as Chef James." He sat up. "I'm the chef at J. J's. I need to get out of here and get back to work."

Billy came over. "I'm Billy, and this is Thomas. We're stuck on a slave ship and it doesn't look like any of us are goin' anywhere." Chef James passed out once again and Billy gently laid his head down onto the floor.

CHAPTER FIVE
March 4, 1859

On the day of the journey, Foster and Taney met at the ship at noon with seventeen paid crewmen. Foster began utilizing his role as captain by barking orders to the crew. "You men, get those barrels loaded!"

Taney joined in. "Stage the cargo over there in plain sight." They loaded plenty of barrels of palm oil on the top deck. Because the large amount of provisions on board was obviously more than what a crew of their size needed, the extra food and water were hidden under boards in the base of the ship or in barrels. Large amounts of gold and goods—cloth, crockery, liquor, knives, cigars, iron bars, guns, gunpowder—were onboard to exchange for slaves. Much of this cargo, too, had to be hidden. More experienced sailors tested the anchor and sails to prepare the ship for hoisting and cast off. Soon the crew grew tired, and some sat down while others stood taking in the breeze from the bay.

Captain Foster stood with authority at the bow of the ship with all hands on deck except for the shanghaied ones below. Seeing the men slack off, Foster cupped his hands around his mouth and shouted, "Get back to work, the lot of you! Move the rest of those crates until they are stored and hidden from sight!" He turned to Taney, who stood beside him. "Your job as first mate is to keep control of the men and make sure they always stay in line. You must ensure that everything is in good working order," he said in a serious tone.

"Don't worry; I will make sure everything runs smoothly. It might be difficult to watch over all of the crew, but I will do my best. I know I will need help when we bring the slaves aboard."

"I know you will. As for the return journey, my own slave driver, Mr. Lasher will be coming with us to assist you. He will keep everything in order."

That afternoon, Meaher met with Foster and Taney on the ship's deck to ensure that everything was going as planned. Meaher handed Foster final instructions. "What time are you pulling out?

"We will depart at dusk," Foster replied. Meaher shook hands with Foster and Taney, wished them a safe journey, and left the ship. "I am leaving too and will be back before dusk," Foster told Taney. "Make final preparations for sail." He could see the men working on the ship as he walked down the plank onto the dock.

Five o'clock that evening, Taney was still hard at work securing large barrels on the top deck. He looked up and saw several crewmen looking in one direction. He turned to look and saw Foster walking onto the ship with a slave girl in tow. Taney's eyes widened as he recognized the girl. Foster had brought the slave girl with the diamonds right to him! From that moment he could think of nothing more than getting his hands on them.

The slave girl with Captain Foster was trembling with fear as she walked past the pungent crew. Some men stared. Others roared encouragement and offered vulgar suggestions. Foster interrupted their taunting, yelling, "Let me have your attention! This is my slave, Nia. She is joining us on the journey. If anyone offends her in any way, I will have your head and feed your body to the sharks! Taney, I expect that you will repeat this information to every man this ship!" He walked slowly down the line of crewmen, his eyes boring into each man in turn. The crew stayed quiet.

Taney observed this display, his eyes on the girl. This was the first opportunity that Taney had had to be near Nia since learning of the diamonds. His stomach twisted, his palms became clammy, and his heart started to pound at the thought of getting his hands on her diamonds.

Foster took Nia's hand, leading her toward the cabins. She crossed her free arm over her chest as they walked past the crew. When she neared Taney, he reached out and cupped his hands around her hips, feeling for the diamonds in her pockets. His quick search revealed nothing. With his hands still on her hips he jokingly asked, "Are you keeping the cargo in fine shape, Captain?"

"Hands off!" Foster cried, whirling around and pushing his fists into Taney's chest until he had him against the side of the ship. His display of anger surprised Taney in spite of his earlier speech. Foster gripped Taney's neck, practically lifting him off his feet. "Mr. Taney," he growled, "What I said to the rest of the crew goes for you, too. If you so much as touch her again, I shall hang you from the crow's nest. Is that clear?"

"Aye, sir," Taney choked out.

Foster eased him back down to his feet, and released his hands from Taney's throat.

"I didn't think that a slave would mean that much to you," Taney grumbled putting his hands up in surrender. He straightened his clothes and smiled thinly.

Foster ignored the comment. "Come, Nia," he said, leading her away from the now silent crowd.

He led her down a narrow passageway. "I am going to place you in my private quarters." Foster pulled a cord with a key on it from his neck, unlocked a door and ushered her inside. As he stepped in, he placed the key back around his neck and tucked it inside his shirt. "This will be your home for the length of the journey. I think you will be comfortable here." Foster noticed that Nia was still shaken from the events on deck. "I'm going to lock you in to keep away the vulgar ship hands," he assured her.

"Thank you, sir," she said, and Foster stepped out, closing the door behind him. She heard the door lock from the other side and felt safer.

She looked around the cabin. A bed filled one corner and a big table dominated the middle of the room with a candle, lantern, maps, and a spyglass on top of it. Two chairs sat at the table. Although the cabin was spacious with furniture much nicer than Nia was used to, it had a damp, stale smell.

She walked over to a small round window and stared out into the bay that flowed into the deep blue sea. The rocking of the boat brought back memories of the boat that had brought her to America.

Back on deck Captain Foster checked his pocket watch. He shouted, "Prepare to sail!"

There was a flurry of activity as crew climbed up the masts and readied them for departure. Sailors rushed about dropping lines, pulling and uncoiling ropes.

The anchor was raised and the *Clotilda* slowly pulled away from the dock, her sails completely unfurled like enormous sheets hanging out to dry. Enough breezes caught the sails that the *Clotilda* began her path to the sea. As the ship left the bay, the men below deck felt a soothing rocking. The farther from land they sailed, the more the ship rocked, not to be still until they reached their destination.

Sitting on the floor with the other captives, Thomas Fitzpatrick started to feel ill and soon vomited. He wasn't the only one. Cursing seasickness, he pulled himself onto a sack of beans next to the one Billy already occupied. "Looks like we're leaving port! I wonder how long they'll keep us down here," Thomas said.

"Not sure. I'm not sure of anything," Billy responded.

Their first morning at sea Captain Foster asked Mr. Lasher to bring all the men up from below deck. When they arrived on deck, some of them were still feeling the effects of seasickness. They shielded their eyes from the bright sun, needing time to adjust to the light. As they looked around all they could see was the ocean, white clouds, blue sky, and Mobile in the distance. They were brought before Foster.

"I am Captain Foster," he told them. "What I say is law. You men have been chosen to go to Africa and help run this ship."

"You have no right to do this to us," Thomas yelled. "I demand that you take us back to Mobile."

Foster nodded to Mr. Lasher, and the tall, rough-looking White man walked up to Thomas with Foster following slowly behind. Foster stopped in front of Thomas. "You want to go back to Mobile, you say?"

"Yes, I do. I don't know what you guys are up to, but this is unlawful. It's kidnapping, and I will have your head for this," Thomas stated forcefully.

Mr. Lasher grabbed Thomas by his shirt collar and belt, picked him up, and slammed him into the ship's rail. He lifted Thomas from the deck and threw him overboard into the cold blue ocean. Following the splash, the men heard Thomas's desperate screams for help. The ship continued to onward, and the screams faded. The remaining men stood in stunned silence.

"Does anyone else want to go back to Mobile?" Captain Foster inquired darkly.

There was no reply.

Foster turned to Mr. Lasher and said, "The loud-mouthed ones never work out; they are more trouble than they are worth."

Mr. Lasher nodded. "It is just as well he is gone."

Foster faced the remaining men with a stern countenance. "You men are part of this crew. This is going to be hard work for most of you. If you do what you're told, you will survive the journey without incident and will be paid a small sum. Those of you who decide not to work," he added, "will be dealt with severely. You are dismissed."

They went below to the berth deck to find a place with the rest of the crew. They were put near the bow of the ship, where it was tight and cramped.

After watching several other sailors get into hammocks, the captured men positioned themselves into theirs. The ship groaned and creaked and rolled. Billy knew it would take some getting used to. He could hear constant snoring and occasional explosive flatulence. Struggling into a sitting position, he wondered how anyone could sleep through these noises that overrode the sounds of the ship. Finally, he lay back down and put his hands over his ears. Thomas Fitzpatrick kept coming to his mind. They hadn't known each other long, but Thomas had treated him well. Billy didn't think he'd ever forget the sound of his cries for help. With his stomach twisting—whether from the rolling of the ship or from fear, Billy wasn't sure—he finally fell into a fitful sleep.

On the second day at sea Captain Foster and Captain Taney stood on deck as Lasher brought the captured crewmen before them.

Captain Foster started with the young Black man on the end. "I believe we met outside the Devil's Tavern," he said. "Billy, was it? I am Captain Foster and this is First Mate Taney. We will be assigning your duties on this journey. You told me you were a ship carpenter at some point in your life."

"Yes I was, sir," Billy answered. "I worked with my father for years on a cargo ship. He taught me everything about being a carpenter. But why did you kidnap me?"

Ignoring his question, Foster responded, "I will need you to keep a close eye on the ship's condition at all times. You will be paid for the work you do on our journey to Africa."

"Africa! I cannot go to Africa," Billy said desperately, and others in line reacted to the news of their destination. "I have a mamma to care for. You can't force us to do this! I'm a free man and I got my papers to prove it. I demand that you turn this ship around."

"Billy, let me make myself very clear. You may be a free Black, but you will either do this quietly or we can do this the hard way." Lasher stepped up to Billy.

"What do you need for me to do?" Billy asked quietly.

"Good then. I thought you would see things my way. First, I want you to work with the crew to build walls below deck to separate the male slaves from the female slaves. We don't need any slave women becoming pregnant and ill on this journey."

Billy was dismissed to begin work, along with several crew assigned to him. After they completed the walls, they also built platforms halfway between the first and second decks. There wasn't enough space for Billy to stand up straight between the decks, and as he crouched there, installing shelves only two and one-half feet apart, he tried not to think about those who would soon occupy the space.

The days passed quickly, and by the seventh day at sea the crewmen were no longer seasick, though the ship continued to toss up and down and sideways on the sea. Like a living thing, the ship constantly rolled with the waves and the men learned to sway with it.

With food tightly rationed several of the crew decided to fish for their supper. That evening they sat in the galley eating their catch. Fresh fish was a nice change from beans and salted pork.

After washing the fish down with ale, some of the crew began to sing. Billy sat off to the side by himself. Life on board the ship was not great, but it was manageable. He missed his mama. He knew she must be extremely worried about him and wondered how she was getting along without him.

On the eighth day small dark clouds appeared overhead and caused some concern among the veterans in the crew. Captain Foster and Mr. Lasher moved across the deck and approached the rail where Taney and several of the men were talking as they looked out at the horizon. "Looks like there is a big storm brewing," Taney said.

"Yes," Foster agreed. The clouds are getting darker by the minute and the winds are picking up. I've been through a few of these. It's going to be a rough ride. Get your men in place and prepare the ship according to plan. Take six of your men and make sure that the ship is battened down. The food should be extra-secure, double-roped, and covered," Foster ordered.

"Aye," Taney replied.

"Everyone who can be spared should go below deck to rest up. When the storm hits, we may need all hands on deck," Captain Foster added.

After several of the men had gathered, Taney proceeded to assign tasks according to Foster's orders.

Some of the men went down to the berth deck to rest, and others scurried around the ship pulling and tightening ropes, moving cargo into secured areas, and retying the loads above and below deck. Some went up the main mast to furl the sails, leaving just the top gallants out to provide steering for what was to come.

As the winds cooled and the waves grew rougher, a sense of urgency flowed through the crew. Men lost their balance as the wind buffeted them and the waves crashed over them. They held onto a rope or rail, using one hand to complete their task. Everyone's life depended on being prepared. For the first time on the journey, Foster could see how well the men worked together in a crisis and was pleased.

Dark clouds blocked the last of the sunlight. Lightning flashed across the sky and cracks of thunder followed. The direction and speed of the wind currents meant the storm was heading their way.

"We're almost done!" shouted Taney to Captain Foster.

Just then a bolt of lightning erupted from the clouds and a heavy gust of wind sprayed the crew with salt water and shifted the *Clotilda*'s direction. As the mast shifted, the men on deck heard a scream. Searching for the source of the sound, they saw that one of the crewmen had fallen out of the mast hold. He was tied to a rope, dangling in the gusting wind over the open seas. Taney instructed six men to pull in the rope with a long hook. Within minutes, the men had pulled their fallen crewmate to safety.

"We have to hurry. It will get much worse soon—you men get these sails furled!" Taney yelled. "And somebody get the rest of the crew up here promptly and tell Billy to get up here to check out the ship!"

The wind increased and lightning split the clouds. The ship was at the mercy of the rolling sea, and the crew had done all it could. Cold, dark waves washed over the deck of the ship, and the crew and Captain Foster had to tie themselves to the rigging to keep from being slammed against the bulwarks or washed overboard.

As Billy and the rest of the crew joined them, a mountainous wave crashed onto the deck and pushed the ship sideways. One seaman flew through the air and went overboard, but the rope tied around his waist and shoulder drew him back onboard as the ship straightened. All the men could do was hang on for their lives and hope God would see them through.

Foster wondered how Nia was fairing in the storm. He released the rail and ran to his cabin. Taney saw him go, but did not dwell on it as the ship pitched again.

When Foster managed to unlock his cabin door he found Nia standing in a corner holding onto the bed frame. It stood only two feet high, but it was the most secure thing in the room since it was hammered into the floorboards. Papers, bedding, and pieces of a broken lamp were among the jumble on the floor tossing with each wave. Foster crossed the room and put his arms around Nia. She held onto him tightly and he could feel her trembling. "It will be over soon," he murmured. "I promised you that I would always take care of you, Nia, through mother-nature storms and through the storms of life." They stood together a moment longer, and then he drew back. "You are in the safest place possible. Just keep holding on. I must go back to the crew, but I will be back when I can," he said.

As the storm subsided on the tenth day at sea, Foster ordered most of the men to get food and rest. By the fourteenth day, the storm had completely passed and the sunshine shone over the ship.

Foster and Taney met on deck to view the damages from the storm.

"The nightmare is over. Once again the *Clotilda* faired very well through a harsh storm," Foster said with pride.

Billy approached. "Excuse me, Captain. There is some damage to the rigging. You will need to send some men up the cable ladders to the spars that held the sails. Fortunately, the mast and spars had survived intact, so little repair is needed."

Foster ordered a crewman to climb up to the crow's nest to oversee repairs. When the task was done, he took out a scope and placed it to his left eye. He looked out at the sea, turning his body in a complete circle. Something caught his eye and he took a second look. "Sail ho! Off the starboard side," he yelled down to the deck.

Immediately, Foster, Taney, and all available crew rushed to the starboard side to have a look. Only a blur of white sails was visible, where gray skies met the sea. Captain Foster positioned himself under the crow's nest, squinted at the crewman fifty feet above, and called, "What kind of ship is she?"

"A frigate, Captain, showing three main masts," he yelled back.

Foster turned to Taney. After a brief discussion they

broke apart calling to the crew, "All hands on deck! Set full sail!"

As the crewman climbed down from his station, he asked Taney, "Why are we setting full sail?"

"You never want to meet up with a warship," Taney said. "They will often take part of a ship's crew to fill their own losses. We would be at their mercy," he admitted, shaking his head. "We can hope we are not seen, as a frigate has greater speed than we do. If we can keep out of their range until dark, we can give them the slip then." Taney glanced back in the direction of the oncoming warship. "Go back up and take a second look."

The crewman resumed his position in the crow's nest. "It's too late, Captain Taney! We've been spotted and they're closing in on us!" he yelled. He kept Captain Foster apprised of the progress of the ship. Too soon, Foster and Taney could see the frigate in their own scopes. The Union Jack of the British Navy flew from her mast. A mile separated the ships, with about an hour of light left.

"It is going to be close," Foster said to Taney.

"Will they try to sink us?" Captain Taney asked.

"One can never know what the British will do. They think the seas are their own. You can be sure that they will try to do something for their own benefit, not ours."

As dusk fell, the British frigate opened fire with its long gun.

"My God!" Billy yelled. "They're firing at us."

The crew could see a long puff of smoke, but the warship was out of range, and the shot fell short of the *Clotilda*. They made another attempt and fell short once again.

"Keep the sail sturdy, men!" Foster yelled. "Clearly, the coming darkness has affected the warship's target capabilities," he announced with satisfaction.

An hour passed, and the *Clotilda* maintained a safe distance from the frigate. Captain Foster announced with some relief, "We're safe for now, but we're still not out of danger completely. Taney, instruct your men to keep all lanterns off and to not even light a pipe. Chef James, you will have to prepare meals without fire. Any flame or smoke could give away our position.

"There will be a game of cat and mouse throughout the night, and we must continue to give them the slip."

When darkness had fallen, Captain Foster took a position on the forecastle. There was still no sign of the British ship. Using a hooded light, he took readings with his sextant, attempting to discover how far they had been driven off course by the storm. He calculated the necessary adjustments and advised Taney to steer south.

Foster returned to his private quarters to write in the ship's log before turning in for the night. Nia had returned everything to order and lay in his bed not yet asleep. Foster stood over Nia and gazed at her for a long time. She felt his presence and turned over to find him staring at her.

"What is it, Mister Foster?" she asked, beginning to sit up.

"Don't—just stay right there, Nia. Let me look at you just the way you are. I…I think that it is time to share with you something I have been feeling for some time." Foster he sat down next to her.

"Yes, sir," Nia replied, her heart beating faster. She knew that it was wrong for a White man to have a relationship with an African slave, but she knew they shared a special bond, and not just because she interpreted his dreams with her sacred stones. There was more, she knew, but she needed to hear Foster tell her himself.

"Nia, I—"

A sharp knock at the door caused them both to jump. "Sir, I am sorry to bother you," came a muffled voice, "but you are needed on deck."

Foster sighed heavily and stood up. Without a word to Nia, he left the room and locked her in. Walking away he thought about what had just happened. He was almost glad for the interruption, so confused was he by his own feelings. He did not know how to express his feelings to Nia. Nor did he know how he would live with her if he did confess. As he continued to walk away, he shook his head and convinced himself not to confess his feelings to her.

Predawn brought clear skies. The crewman was again sent aloft as the sky lightened. His stomach twisted as he wondered whether he would see the British warship. Perched in the crow's nest, he quickly made a full circle and saw nothing close by. He continued his watchfulness until the sun had fully risen. With relief he called down, "All clear! There is nothing in sight!"

CHAPTER SIX

Kingdom of Dahomey, Africa

A beautiful and very intelligent young woman named Areba was shopping in the village marketplace near the city of Tamale. She looked at a pile of mangoes and remembered how much her sister loved to eat them.. Nia had been ten years old when a rival tribe took her while she was picking berries in the woods. Areba had heard that Nia was sold by that rival tribe to a White man in America. That had been three years ago.

Looking around to make certain no one was watching, Areba pulled from her headpiece three stones wrapped in a gele. Carefully, she unwrapped them and implored quietly. "Why don't you lend your sacred powers and bring my sister back to me?" She placed them gently back into the gele on her head.

Areba veered through the apples and mangoes and saw a tall, handsome man standing and whittling. As she came closer she could see small and well-defined African Royalty pieces made from wood.

She was intrigued by the pieces she saw, but she was more intrigued with him. He is a beautiful figure of God's own art, she thought, and she stood fantasizing about him until she was jostled from behind.

"Oh, pardon me," the women said to Areba.

"It's all right," Areba said, awakened from her fantasy. She finished her shopping and went home.

The next day, she visited the marketplace again, fumbling over fruit as if she were picking the best pieces. Once again, she found the opportunity to watch the handsome man through the rows of fruit. Areba anxiously wanted to meet him, but was too shy to start a conversation, so she browsed closer and closer to him hoping that he would notice her. He did.

"Hello, Miss..."

"Oh, my name is Areba. Hello," she responded looking away shyly.

"Did you find what you are looking for?" he asked.

"Well...uh I have. I'm just picking some fruit for my family."

"Forgive my rudeness. I have not introduced myself. My name is Jabar," he said as he moved closer and bowed to greet her properly.

"It is very nice meeting you Jabar," she said as her heart pounded. He was even more handsome up close.

"May I interest you in some lunch Miss Areba?" Jabar asked.

"I...I would love to, but I must get back to work," she said. "Perhaps we can have lunch some other time. I am sure I will see you again. I shop at this marketplace often."

"I know you do," he said with a devilish smile. "I see you every time you come in here, and it has been a pleasure each and every time."

Areba felt her cheeks heat up. "Well, Jabar good day."

"Good day to you Miss…Areba!"

Areba found a reason to go to the marketplace the next day and the next, and Jabar visited with her each time. By the next week they found time away from work and chores to court and enjoy every free moment together. They took long walks in open fields and shared their affection with the open skies.

On one such day, Jabar turned to Areba and took her hand. "Areba, I know that we've only known one another for four weeks, but I am in love with you, and want to make you my wife," he said earnestly.

"Oh, my Jabar, I am in love with you too," she answered. "But before we make plans, you know that you must meet my family and ask my father for my hand."

"Then I must meet them tomorrow," Jabar announced. She looked in his eyes and smiled.

The next evening after Jabar finished work, he met with Areba and her family, and asked for her hand in marriage. Areba's father was delighted and gave his permission. Jabar ran home, joy carrying him faster than he'd ever gone, to share the news with his own family.

The next day, as was their cultural tradition Jabar was escorted by his family to Areba's home for the marriage ceremony. When Jabar and his family arrived, they were greeted by Areba, her mother and father, two aunts, cousins, and a priest. When Jabar's family entered Areba's home, they kneeled to show respect for her family. The two families sat on opposite sides of a colorful woven rug, Areba and Jabar sitting in the center of the family circle.

Jabar's mother walked over to Areba's family, her arms full of gifts that reinforce what is desirable and necessary to make a marriage and, indeed, life itself successful.

"The first gift we present to you is honey," she began. "The quality of honey is sweetness. May your married life be sweet and happy, blessed with many children and money to take care of them. The second is salt. It preserves. May you be preserved in your lives so that you live long and see your children's children. The third gift is palm oil. It reduces the harsh taste of pepper in the soup. May the harsh impact of difficult times be lessened. The fourth item is the kola nut." She turned to Jabar with a smile. "It makes your wife as fertile as the kola nut tree and blesses her with many children who survive and do great things in life." Everyone chuckles at the presentation. "Fifth and last, we present this rooster and a small gift of money."

As Jabar's mother finished, Areba took the rooster and presented it to her mother. Everyone cheered at Areba's acceptance of Jabar.

Jabar walked over to Areba's father.

"I will perform a number of duties for your family, sir," he said. "I will weed your farm, thatch your leaking roof, and help you with harvest."

"I gladly accept your help," Areba's father replied. "We will get started soon."

Two of Areba's cousins began thumping on decorative hour-glass shaped talking drums, Jabar kissed his new bride, and the two families began dancing around Areba and Jabar in celebration. Family members and priest alike partook of delicious food and drink.

It was the happiest day of Areba's life. Little did she know that the *Clotilda* was sailing her way and would change her life forever.

After the ceremony Areba walked to her and Jabar's new home, closely situated near her parents' home. Jabar stayed a while longer talking to their families while Areba prepared for him. Still dressed in her wedding clothes, Areba sat alone on the bed. She had never felt so happy, but her happiness wavered when she thought about Nia. She sat looking up at the ceiling wishing she could share this moment of happiness with her sister.

She pulled the stones from her gele. The visions came immediately, visions of someone abducting her. Areba heard Jabar coming and tucked the stones away.

Later that night, Areba lay asleep in Jabar's arms. She awoke suddenly to her own screams, sitting up in the bed and pulling away from her husband as she pulled away from those who chased her in her nightmare. Jabar sat up next to Areba.

"What is it, my darling?" Jabar asked.

Areba breathed in and out, trying to calm herself. "It is just a bad dream. I will try to go back to sleep," she said.

Areba lay in the bed with her eyes open thinking about Nia and wondered why the White man wanted so many African people. Based on the visions her sacred stones gave her, she knew it was only a matter of time before she would also be captured.

Areba knew about the rivalries that arose among neighboring tribes. They fought for the most sought after commodity—people. She had heard stories about the Dahomey Tribe, especially the female soldiers who were fierce and were said to capture tribes with muskets, machetes, and if need be, with their own bare teeth. Areba wondered if the stories were true. Finally, she rested her head on her husband's shoulder and fell into a worried sleep.

One very hot evening not long after her wedding, Areba collected water on the riverbank in the Yoruba's Tartar Village near the city of Tamale. As she flung a rope tied to a bucket filled with water over her shoulder, two large women approached her.

"Hello," one woman said in the Yoruba language.

"Hello," Areba replied.

"Would you like to trade some goods?" the other woman asked. "We have fruits and vegetables. What do you have to trade?"

"I only have water, but if you would like to come to my village, there are many items to trade," Areba answered. The women looked around. "My village is that way," Areba said, pointing north. The tall women looked at Areba and looked around once again.

Areba realized there were many more women hiding in the bushes nearby. *Dahomey*, she thought, fear gripping her. Before she could react several large Dahomey warrior women darted toward her and grabbed her arms, dragging her with much force. She kicked, punched, and screamed for the other villagers in a nearby field, but her friends and family were too far away to hear her. The women dragged her until her feet and knees bled.

A large regiment of Dahomey warriors wearing crocodile hide headdresses and carrying shields and spears entered Areba's village, filling it with the sound of tribal singing, chanting, and drumbeats.

A group of Dahomey warriors grappled with several Yorubians capturing them. Spears flew, shields clanked, and the sound of the children's horrified screams echoed through the darkness.

Areba, restrained with the other captives, heard constant screaming in the air. She thought of her mother, father, and Jabar. "Oh my Olorun, most high God! Please protect my mama!"

"Mama! Mama!" she yelled, trying to fight off the strong women. Finally, after a long struggle, Areba fell limp. She was helpless against the strength of the large women holding onto her.

Areba watched as the fittest and most able members of her community were taken by the Dahomey. The young and strong were chained together by their necks, and were marched closely behind Areba. The old, the very young, and the unfit were left behind or killed in the burning village.

The visions she'd had on the night of her wedding were fulfilled that night. She had been captured to be a slave, but to whom?

For two days, Areba and hundreds of other villagers were prodded through rough jungles. Areba's whole body hurt and her throat felt parched. Dizzily, she felt for the stones through her gele. She stumbled and collapsed on the ground, unable to go on.

"Get up!" one of the Dahomey soldiers yelled. When Areba remained there, unmoving, the soldier leaned down and placed her finger under Areba's nose. When she could feel that Areba was still breathing, she picked her up and flung her over her shoulder, continuing the journey.

As Areba drifted into unconsciousness, her mind took her to a moment from her childhood.

It was hot summer day in the Tartar Village. Areba and Nia were sitting with their mama, Monika, and several other women, just outside of the village near the river's edge. The women sat in a circle telling stories of the past as they weaved straw baskets and sorted lentils. One older woman shushed the others and began telling another story.

"Many of you younger women and girls will love this story," she said. "It is about the sacred stones. Over fifty years ago, two sisters found some very bright and shining stones near the water's edge. After finding them, the sisters' lives changed.

"The sacred stones allowed the sisters to understand dreams and see visions of the future, but this gift wasn't always a welcome one. Many in the village envied their power and some demanded to know about their own future. Men tried to seduce them and women with sick children begged them to use the power of the stones for healing. One man tried to steal the stones from one of the girls as she was collecting water for her family. He stole them and ran along the riverbank, but as he ran away, he tripped and fell, and cut his leg so badly that he bled to death. The stones were flung into the water. Many tried to find the stones, but they have never been found.

"Those stones will reveal themselves only to the ones who were meant for them, and once the stones are united with the intended people, they will have great powers to do wonderful things for their people. The stones are somewhere out there now, waiting for the right ones."

Areba and Nia were intrigued. They looked at one another and snuck away from the circle of women.

"I wish I had those sacred stones so that I could have powers. I would fill the village with fish and fruit," said Areba to Nia.

"It sure would be a stinky village," Nia said. Both girls laughed and held hands, walking toward the river. "I'm going to find the stones!" Nia announced.

"No, I'm going to find them!" said Areba. Giggling, the girls reached the riverbank and began crawling on their hands and knees, digging through the sand.

After ten minutes, Nia sat back on her heels. "I'm tired of looking for the stones," she said.

"Me too. Those stones probably don't exist anymore or the fishes swallowed them. Let's play!" Areba jumped up and tagged Nia then ran into the water. Nia followed Areba, laughing and splashing her. They raised their dresses and slowly walked into the chilly water until it reached Nia's knees. The women could hear their laughter and Monika turned to check on them periodically.

The girls walked downriver toward a big rock that stood fifteen feet out of the water. Nia paused to look at the rocks and shells near her feet. Areba continued forward to the towering rock.

Something sparkled there, embedded in the large rock. The nearer she came, the brighter it seemed to glisten in the sunlight. As she drew closer, the water grew deeper. Areba reached out her hand and brushed her fingers over the sparkling stones. She counted five of them, small enough to fit in her palm. Captivated by the stones, she could not look away. She felt a force pulling her toward them. The force drew her in and she cried out before going into a trance.

Nia stood up, a shell in her hand, and saw her sister standing in the deep water. "Areba! Come back," she yelled. All of a sudden, a large wave washed over Areba. The waves were continual now that the tide was coming in.

When Areba did not respond, Nia knew that her sister was in trouble. "Mama, Mama! Help!" Nia yelled, struggling to stay upright as the waves reached her.

Monika looked up and only saw Nia standing in the water. Then her eyes found Areba, standing in deep water by the large rock, overcome by waves. She jumped up swiftly and ran toward the water.

"Areba!" she yelled as she ran across the sandy ground and into the chilly waters. She moved past Nia toward Areba, who stood still in the waves.

"What is wrong with you, girl? Get out of that water!" Monica demanded. Areba did not answer. "Areba!" Monica called once more. She reached her daughter and took hold of her arm, but could not budge her. Something was holding Areba to that spot.

Monika yelled, "Help, I cannot move her!" The village women ran into the water toward the pair. Monika pulled at Areba frantically and yelled, "Let my Areba go!"

Several women joined Monika, trying to pull Areba from the unseen force. The women struggled until they were exhausted. They took Nia to the bank and stood watching Monika become more and more frantic as she and Areba were constantly overtaken by the waves. Monika stood over Areba in the water crying and praying to her God. Finally, the unseen force that held Areba let her go.

Monika grabbed Areba from the water and pulled her to her chest. She struggled to the shallow water and collapsed, holding Areba so close that she could feel her heart pounding. Nia huddled next to her mother and sister, and the others stood by watching.

Monika could see that Areba was clutching something. "What do you have there?" she asked, opening Areba's hands. The women peered over Monika's shoulder.

"The sacred stones!" an elderly woman yelled. Everyone looked at the stones and then at Areba with amazement. "She's the chosen one!" the woman proclaimed.

"That can't be," Monica said as she looked at the stones with wide eyes.

"What, Mama?" Areba asked, still dazed.

"Let me take a closer look, Areba."

The old woman spoke again. "Beware that the powers you will possess will be plenty. Everyone will have questions for you, but they may not like what you have to say. Just speak the truth." The old woman smiled. "It is tradition to celebrate the chosen one," she said. "I will help you with the celebration, Monika."

"Well…I…we will speak of celebrations later," Monika said. She took the stones from Areba's hand, wrapped them in a piece of cloth, and placed them in her waist pouch.

"You girls come with me," Monika said, getting to her feet. She helped Areba up and held her hand, taking Nia's with the other. All of the women still stood in the water looking at them and whispering about what they had just seen.

Monika walked to the bank with her daughters and headed down a path to the village. The walk home was quiet, but when they arrived at their hut, Monika sat down with the girls to tell them more about the stones and the powers Areba now possessed.

"Those stones you found today were not just rocks—they are sacred stones that provide special powers from the gods," she said.

"Like the stones in the story? Areba really found them?" Nia asked. Monika nodded. "Where did they come from, Mama?" The girls leaned in to hear the response.

"The stones were fragments from the stars that fell from the heavens many hundreds of years ago. And just as the story said, the person or persons who found them would be the chosen ones to lead the tribe to prosperity. The stones would give them special powers to foresee the future and read dreams.

"Two sisters had these stones and the villagers relied on them tremendously to interpret dreams. They believed that the interpretations would help them make decisions and forewarn them of danger to come. The sisters also had visions that showed them the future, but they could not make these visions come true. They had to be open to the stones and their power, and it was a great responsibility.

"Areba, now that you have the sacred stones, you are the chosen one. You must keep these sacred stones with you wherever you go." Monika took out her waist pouch. "Keep them hidden inside of this pouch and tuck the pouch inside of your gele," Monika said. She tucked the pouch inside of Areba's gele while Nia looked on.

"Treasure the stones and guard them with your life, and one day you will be able to read dreams and help our tribe to do things the gods want you to do," Monika said. She looked into her daughter's eyes and smiled.

That night Areba took the stones out of the pouch her mother gave to her. Nia sat next to her sister and looked at the stones.

"Can I have a stone and have special powers too?" Nia asked.

"Yes, I will share with you, Nia." Areba grabbed Nia's hand, placed two stones in her palm and folded her hands over Nia's. "Now you will have the power too," she said.

The girls embraced. Holding her sister tightly, Areba whispered, "Let's promise to always be together and never let anything separate us."

"I promise," Nia replied.

CHAPTER SEVEN

Areba woke from her fainting spell. She opened her eyes and sat straight up. She found herself in a dark room, and she was not alone. There were many familiar faces from her village, but she also heard whispers in many languages and saw that some did not display the Yoruba markings on their faces or chests. Everyone was chained together.

She could see from a crack in the wall that the large wooden building had tall gates surrounding it. Very little light came through the cracks and the room felt damp, the air salty. Areba wondered where she had been taken, but she could not ask those next to her.

Jabar was also herded through the woods along with other men. His hunger and thirst were extreme, hardly assuaged by the pittance he was fed by his captors. He wondered if he would ever see his home and family again.

Eventually his captors took him through tall gates and into a huge wooden building. As he walked through the captured Africans, his eyes set on a beautiful woman with light eyes—Areba!

"Areba!" he yelled, struggling against the binding at his wrists. One of the warriors hit him over the head with something hard and marched him onward. On the other side of the room he recognized those from his village by the markings on their faces. The fear on their faces matched his own. Other than calling out his wife's name, he had not spoken a word since his capture. The only sound that came from him was the growling of his hungry belly.

For weeks, Areba crouched in a corner of the building chained to several others. Twice per day they were given a bit of food and water. The building was kept extremely dark even during daylight. Areba did not know then that the captives were kept in the dark so they would be prepared for the darkness in the ship's hull.

Although Jabar was nearby, Areba never saw him. She yearned to be with him and cried silently at night. She knew that she could not cry out because the villagers were beaten for making the slightest sound.

Some men and women were beaten for attempting to free themselves from the chains. Others became very ill from the dampness. In spite of the guards and the dreadful conditions, the captives began to bond even though many of them spoke in a different tongue. Some spoke multiple languages and they were able to interpret during conversations when the warrior women were not around. In whispers, they wondered how they could escape.

A middle-aged African woman shared rumors that White people would eat them. Another woman shared her belief that what they were experiencing was just a dream and that it would end soon. There were many rumors going around the old building, but Areba did not believe any of them. She wondered what lay ahead but could not imagine the nightmare that awaited her.

"On your feet!" The slaved driver cracked his whip against the floor. The guards herded Areba and the rest of the women out of the darkness and into the light. Everyone stumbled, not used to walking, and cowered against the brightness. The men followed, pushed roughly along. Areba caught sight of Jabar and her heart pounded with excitement. Their eyes connected. A message passed between them. Everything is going to be all right. I love you. The guards gathered everyone in groups around large tubs of water and poured buckets of water over them to wash off the stench. Their unused muscles ached from the movement, and their eyes could barely focus.

Next the guards rubbed palm oil into their skin. Tears rolled down Areba's face from the humiliation she felt as the Dahomey women pawed her roughly before moving on. She watched as they moved down the line, and shared the indignity of the other women as they were touched in the most private areas.

Areba and the others, bodies glistening in the sun, were led with hands and feet tied to one another to a trading post at the edge of the open sea. The Dahomey guards led the captives to a massive wooden platform and told several of them to climb up the steps.

Areba saw a ship in the distance and several small boats pulled up on the shore, loaded with White men. One Black man and one Black woman were with them.

On the shore, Captain Foster, Nia, Taney, Billy and some of the crew stepped out of the small boats and made their way to the trading post. Three hundred Dahomey women warriors, the Dahomey Chief, and a Brazilian named Don Francisco, whom the chief had hired to run the trading post, greeted them.

Nia was familiar with the Dahomey women warriors, but Foster was astounded and a bit intimidated by them. He had heard from his father that these women were incredibly strong and frightening, but the description did not fully capture the sight before him. He was amazed by the warriors' masculine physiques but tried to appear unfazed by their considerable stature and piercing stares. Then he caught sight the jawbones of enemies that hung from the women's waists. He and Taney glanced at each other, drawing themselves up to their full height. Billy and the other crewmen stood nearby, trying to take their cues from their captain and first mate, but were unable to look the women warriors in the eye.

Nia stood apart from the men. It took all her strength not to fall to her knees and sink her hands into the African soil. For a moment, she wondered how she could run into the nearby trees so she could stay in Africa where she belonged, but she knew that Foster would never give up until he found her. Her legs shook, whether from being on solid ground after so many weeks on water, or from joy at being home again she could not tell. Her eyes were drawn to her people, tied together up on the platform, where she herself had been three years ago. For a moment she could not trust her sight. Her sister stood there! "Areba," she whispered. Her heart pounded and her hand went to the stones. "Sister, look at me. I am here."

Areba turned and looked into the group where Nia stood. Their eyes met. Tears sprang to Areba's eyes and her throat ached. Nia had returned to her. She had changed so much, grown into a woman. Currents of elation and sorrow flowed between the sisters. To be reunited had been their greatest hope, but reunited under such circumstances their greatest fear.

Don Francisco came up to Foster and introduced himself, turning Foster's attention to the matter at hand. They approached the Dahomey Chief and began bartering. Foster wanted one hundred fifty of the Africans for an equal share of the goods he brought with him.

While the chief examined the goods offered for trade, Foster examined the goods on the platform. He approached a cluster of tall, well-defined men who stared back at him. He assessed their overall health, checking their size, muscles, eyes, and teeth. Foster dismissed those with any obvious infirmity and those who looked too small, weak, or old. Any imperfection rendered them unfit for hard labor.

Foster proceeded to handpick many of the women, who would work both in the fields and in homes. When he had finished looking over all that were present, Foster turned to the Dahomey Chief and agreed to take one hundred twenty-five men, women, and children who appeared older than twelve years.

Taney had his hand at picking a few women to satisfy his own needs. He remembered his maid mentioning that Nia had a sister and that she had diamonds, too. Keeping his exterior calm, he looked at Nia, and then walked slowly past each African woman, carefully studying their features for any resemblance.

When he approached Areba, he paused. He looked again at Nia, then back at Areba. The resemblance was clear to him, and he hid his smile.

While others were busy looking at the Dahomey women and captive Africans, Billy noticed Taney studying Areba. Billy stared at her, too, taking in her beauty. He selfishly and silently hoped that she would be chosen to go to America.

Areba heard the one called Foster ordering the crew to remove some of the men and women from the platform. They were led with force toward the small boats. Areba's worst fears were now confirmed. They were being taken away by the White men. Chaos erupted. The Africans fought back against the White men who pushed and pulled them. The women and children protested loudly in their African languages, trying to run to their men, and the men also tried to reach their families.

Foster turned to an enormous man in black clothing. "Mr. Lasher, show them what happens to those who do not cooperate," he said sternly.

The man nodded and pulled out a gun. Areba shouted, "No!" A shot was fired directly at one of the smaller African men. Everyone witnessed the loud crack of the gun and saw the man, blood pouring from his chest, fall to the ground.

One captive, a medicine man, boldly stepped out of line and crouched over the wounded man. He placed his finger under the man's nose to see if he was breathing. The medicine man looked up slowly and shook his head. The man was dead.

"Get back in line, you old fool!" yelled Lasher.

The Africans were subdued by the murder and were now sufficiently wary of Mr. Lasher. The crewmen started shuffling Africans to the boats. Foster walked along the wooden platform and stopped in front of Areba. She quivered and forced herself not to look at her sister. "I heard you shout when Lasher pulled out the rifle," Foster murmured. He turned to Don Francisco. "Ask her what her name is," he instructed. He did. Areba did not answer. Foster asked again. "What is your name?" Areba looked Foster in the eye but remained silent. "I am going to ask you one more time," Foster said harshly. "What is your name?"

"She doesn't know how to speak English, Captain. She only knows the word, 'no!' What do you expect of these savages!" one crewman sneered. The other crewmen roared with laughter. Areba looked at each of the crewmen, and then she looked at Jabar. Finally, she focused on Foster, staring into his eyes. She spoke with a heavy African accent. "My name is Areba."

The crewmen and the tribal members stared at her with amazement. Foster's eyes widened in surprise and leaned in close, studying her with curiosity. "Meaher is really going to love you, uh—uh Ruba." He gripped her arms roughly and pulled her close to him.

"Hey, you don't have to treat her like that!" Billy yelled. As soon as he'd spoken, he felt a fist across the face.

"Only speak when you are spoken to!" growled Lasher.

Areba spoke again. "My name is Areba," she corrected.

Foster turned to his men. "This is Ruba," he announced. "She's Meaher's, so hands off."

Seeing his wife handled so intimately by the White man, Jabar could not suppress his anger any longer. He pushed his way through the crowd and lunged toward the captain. Lasher moved quickly and raised his rifle, striking Jabar in the head. He crumpled to the ground, unmoving. Within seconds, he was dead.

Areba's anguished yell startled everyone. Foster held her at arm's length as she yelled at all White men in her native language. Billy and Nia were horrified at Lasher's brutality. Tears came to Nia's eyes when she saw her sister's pain. She quickly wiped away the tears, but not before Taney saw them. The obvious connection between the two confirmed to him that they were indeed sisters.

"Jabar was a proud warrior, honorable and loving!" Areba screamed. "He protected his family and tribe. He celebrated his ancestors and the great spirits who looked after them! And now you have killed him! You shall never be forgiven for what you have done and you will pay!" Tears streamed down her face. Foster realized that the dead man meant a great deal to this woman. He had no time for such things. There was much to be done.

The last of Foster's selections were herded to the boats. Many of them were overwhelmed by the vast ocean and wary of the small boats rocking in the waves. As Areba climbed awkwardly into the unfamiliar vessel, she wished she could hold her sacred stones. When they had been made to strip and wash, Areba had kept the stones hidden in their pouch in her gele. She could only pray that she wouldn't be forced to remove her head garment. For now, the stones were safe.

From her place in the boat, squeezed between two others, she looked back at the shore, at Africa. There her husband lay murdered and unburied. There her village and her people had been torn apart. Areba's stomach clenched. The devastation would live with her forever.

The last of the captives climbed into the waiting boat. The sorrow and hatred on the faces of her people were mirrored in Areba's heart. Areba kept her eye on the one called Lasher, the one who had killed her husband. She knew that she would see him pay for what he had done.

The boats rocked across the water and the sun beat down on them. During the short journey to the waiting ship, one man sitting near Areba moaned from the pain of a high fever. Mr. Lasher stood up in the boat and made his way over to the shivering man. "His illness was missed during selection," he announced. "He will not survive the journey." He looked at the crew and jerked his head toward the waves. The crewmen picked him up and dumped him overboard.

Areba and the others gasped in horror, and those in nearby boats turned just in time to see the man begin to sink. Their gasps grew to cries when, as if from nowhere, sharp dorsal fins cut the water. Areba willed herself to turn away as the school of sharks tore into the man. Even the

White men seemed unsettled when the sharks continued to follow the boat, waiting for the next feeding. When the small boats neared the ship, the sharks dropped back and disappeared again. None who had witnessed their meal would soon forget it.

Finally, the *Clotilda* cast her shadow over the approaching boats, providing respite from the scorching sun. One by one, the Africans were hoisted aboard. They climbed up a twenty-foot rope ladder and were greeted by more White men who handled them as though herding cattle. The smaller boats were hoisted and the sails turned to catch the wind.

A barricade separated the officers' quarters from all others, creating a safe area for the captain and first mate in the event the slaves rebelled. Loopholes in the barricade provided a place for the crew to fire their muskets, if needed.

There were two smaller cabins near the captain's cabin. Foster walked over to Areba and took her by the arm. He faced Lasher and said, "This one will go in the small cabin next to mine. She is Meaher's, and no one—no one—is allowed in her cabin. Is that clear?"

"Yes, sir," Lasher responded.

The landmass grew smaller and smaller as the ship traveled farther out to sea. The Africans, now slaves, left their former lives as farmers, fishermen, and traders. There was even some royalty among them. They were from different tribes and different religions, Islam, Vodun, or the Orisa. Some were traditional enemies who became brothers and sisters in servitude. No longer were they mother, father, husband, or wife, but "nigger" and "savage" to the White men.

CHAPTER EIGHT

Although there were some who argued that the African people, too, were created by God in his image, Captain Foster could not be distracted by such questions of morality. He had a job to finish and a bet to win. So he packed his living cargo into the ship, crammed so tightly that they could barely stand.

The stench of disease and human waste filled the cramped space in the hold. The crew fed the slaves very little. They wanted to keep the slaves strong enough to survive, but weak enough that they could not overpower the crew. The slaves were permitted to come on deck for short periods to work their muscles.

Some of the women were made to dance for the crew's entertainment. One particular evening when there was dancing, Areba saw a few of the White men chaining a young girl's hands in front of her and poking at her, pulling at her clothing and grinning at each other. The girl pushed the men's hands away and fought back with a warrior spirit.

Billy was working on a few loose boards at the far end of the deck and couldn't stop himself from glancing at the action. Though he was sorry for the girl, Areba was the one he watched. He hoped that the crew would keep their hands off of her because he knew that he would want to come to her rescue.

Areba shook with anger and disgust that they seemed excited by the girl's aggression. Then the girl reached out and scratched one man across his face. He grabbed his cheek and the other men laughed at their crewmate. He advanced on the girl once more. "You think you can attack me and get away with it?" he asked. He picked her up and strode over to the side of the ship. Areba was horrified when she realized he intended to throw her into the ocean.

Captain Foster appeared on deck just in time to see the man release his grip on the girl. Her screams were silenced when she hit the water.

"That will cost you two week's pay," he said sharply, halting the man's satisfied laughter. "I just paid a precious sum for this lot. We will lose many to illness on this journey. We can't afford to lose more to save your pride. Do I make myself clear?" Foster asked, looking at each of the offending crewmen in turn.

"Yes, Captain," they replied, eyes down.

Foster and his men were surprised to see that even though the slaves spoke various languages and were from different tribes, several groups of four chained together seemed to create strong, tight-knit alliances among themselves. Many crew worried that these alliances could prove dangerous, so Foster made sure the crew monitored the slaves' relationships and continually separated those who seemed to get along too well.

The slaves immediately realized why they were being separated. Whenever the crew came around, they quickly changed their behavior toward one another, appearing aggressive and unfriendly. In this way, they managed to maintain the bonds they formed.

One day, during time on deck, Areba found people from her own tribe chained together near the edge. Winds blew mildly warm salty air through the air and the ship tossed gently on the sea. Separated from the others, as she was in her own cabin, Areba felt immense relief now to have a moment among her people. She found a familiar face, a young man named Kazoola, the Yoruba chief's son. Tall, dark-skinned, and wooly-haired, he spoke several African languages and dialects.

"Kazoola!" Areba said with a smile in the Yoruba language and stooped to fit into the group.

"Areba, I am so glad to see that you are safe," Kazoola replied as he embraced her.

"Yes, I am safe, and it is good to see you are also safe," she replied. "But I feel like a spear has made its way through my heart," she said as tears rolled down her cheeks. "I do not know what happened to my parents. My father was on a hunting trip, but my mother was in the village when the Dahomey attacked."

Kazoola reached over to wipe her tears away and sighed. "At least you did not have to see them die. I watched those animals slash and burn my ailing mother and little brothers and sisters as I was dragged by my feet through the village."

"I'm so sorry, Kazoola." She quickly dismissed any thought of her parents being dead. "I do not know what happened to my parents, but I will pray to see them again until the day I die," she said, taking his hand. "It looks like we are family now. I will look after you like a brother wherever they take us."

"And I will look after you too—my African sister," Kazoola said with a small smile. "Have you ever heard about what happened to your sister Nia? Maybe you will get to see her some day in America."

Areba took a shaky breath. "I do have something good to share." She leaned in and whispered, "God has answered my prayers about seeing my sister again. Nia is here on this ship. She came with the White men."

"What!" Kazoola exclaimed.

"Hush, no one can know."

"I will keep your secret. My heart is glad for you and your sister. The White man first separated you and has now brought you together again. Why do they want us, Areba?" Kazoola asked.

"I heard mumblings from the crew that they are making us their slaves. They are taking us to America to work for those White men," Areba said. Their time on deck came to an end and Areba was taken back to her cabin.

Later that night after dancing, Areba watched Lasher as he stationed himself over the hatch, holding a whip of many twisted thongs in his hand. Whenever he heard the slightest noise below, he pulled a random slave to the deck and whipped him to set an example to the others.

The sharp cracks of the whip and blood-curdling screams were felt by every slave in the hold. Areba knew that they would be in grave danger in America. She felt that the White men behaved even worse than the Dahomey savages. Never before had she seen such brutal cruelty.

Areba was again taken to her cabin with fresh clothing. She wondered why she and Nia were chosen to be treated so differently from the other slaves. She had only seen Nia when they were both on deck with the crew and had not spoken to her. But she had seen her escorted to and from Captain Foster's cabin, right next to her own.

Just then, she realized that when the crew left her earlier that evening, she hadn't heard the door lock. She walked over to the door and slowly turned the knob. The door opened freely. She knew that if she were spotted outside of her cabin that she would see the same fate as the others, but she was willing to take the chance to see Nia. She crept from her cabin. Just as she took a step into the hallway, Foster's door swung inward creaking loudly. Areba quickly stepped backward, her back to the wall, hoping that Foster did not come her way. She heard the sounds of the key in the lock. His footsteps faded in the other direction and she exhaled with relief. With one last look in both directions, she tiptoed to Foster's door. She tapped lightly.

"Nia! It's me, Areba." She heard Nia through the door.

"Sister, you came!" Nia's voice was full of joy as she peeked out of the circular hole in the door. "I cannot open the door," she whispered.

"I know. He locked you inside. I only came to hear your voice and to tell you that I love you, sister. Do not let

Foster know that I am your sister. It seems we both have favor among these White men, and I don't want anything to cause them to alter their ideas about us."

"He will suspect nothing," Nia promised.

"Good night, Nia."

"Good night, Areba."

In the morning, everyone awoke to the sounds of another slave being flogged unmercifully by Lasher. Areba walked around her tiny cabin, willing the beating to stop. Was it someone she knew? She had snuck back to her cabin unnoticed the night before, and her door remained unlocked. Did she dare leave her prison again? Areba eased her door open. What she saw on deck was a man from another tribe, bloodied and barely alive. What had he done that was so horrible? she wondered. The White men stood around him, waiting for him to die. They did not have to wait long. They tossed him over the side as they would have done an animal.

Areba's fear grew with each unfeeling cruelty she saw. She snuck back to her cabin, her stomach twisting with grief. Once inside, she felt for her sacred stones, still hidden safely in the cloth around her head. She gripped the stones in her hand and prayed, for herself and for all who suffered on this ship. Exhausted, she carefully returned the stones to their hiding place and fell asleep, death on her mind.

Throughout each day, the ship rocked and pitched through the waves. The salty sea air, damp, dark quarters and untreated illnesses took a toll on many, even the crew. Diseases passed with lightning speed from one naked body to the next, pressed together as they were. The ship's doctor had endless work, caring for the crew and the slaves.

Alone in her cabin, Areba felt her stomach roll with the waves. She tried to keep herself still on her cot, but the motion never ceased. Terrified, she felt for her stones. She wanted a vision to come, an assurance that this ship would not go under. She clutched the stones in her fist and prayed.

All of a sudden there was light tap on her door. She struggled to keep her balance as she walked over to the door. She slid open the round wood piece at face level and saw a tall, Black man standing there.

"Hello. I am Billy." He smiled at her surprised face. "I am sorry to disturb you Ms. Areba, but I thought that this ginger and water would help you if you are feeling ill."

"Thank you so much, Billy," she said slowly, the English language strange on her tongue. "My stomach feels as though it will never be still. But why would you do me this kindness? Aren't you with the White men?"

"Just like you, I was forced to work on this ship. But to my surprise I am glad that I am here, because I have the opportunity to meet you."

Billy slipped the small cup of liquid through the bars in the round opening. Areba took the cup and threw her head back, quickly swallowing the mixture before it could spill.

"I have to go before I am seen, Areba. I will see you tomorrow. I hope you feel better." Billy's face disappeared.

Suddenly, the ship pitched again and Areba cried out, instinctively reaching her hands out to grab hold of something solid, but she had the cup in one hand and the stones in the other. She lost her balance and the stones tumbled to the floor and skittered across the boards. Areba scrambled after them, restoring two to safety. The third had found its way to a corner, and as Areba tried to reach it, the stone disappeared through a crack. "No!" she gasped. But there was nothing to be done. The stone was gone, whether into the hands of someone below or into the sea, Areba would never know.

They had been at sea two weeks. The weather was calm and the slaves who were healthy enough were to have their time on deck. A member of the crew descended the stairs and began the ritual of unchaining the men from the walls and moving them up the stairs in their tethered groups of four. After all of the men were on deck, the women were allowed to go on deck without chains.

Areba was let out of her cabin. She knew she would not see Nia because she realized that Nia was kept apart from the rest of them. Areba searched instead for Kazoola. She was glad to see he remained well and made her way toward him.

"Kazoola. It gives me happiness to see that you have yet been spared sickness," she said quietly.

"Though I am still strong, many have not been so fortunate. Areba," he said, worry evident in his voice, "I heard some talking below. They plan to end this horror and endure it no longer."

"What? Do they think they can fight the White men? Chained together as they are?"

"I do not know. It was those men there." Kazoola inclined his head slightly, careful not to draw attention.

Areba looked across the deck toward the four men Kazoola had indicated. They stood with their backs to the sea, near the ship's rail.

Foster and Taney stood talking near the group, and Lasher kept a watchful eye on each slave. Areba watched as the four men inched themselves away from Lasher. They walked backwards until their heels met the walls. One of them yelled in his native tongue and then they bent over backwards and flipped overboard. It was over in a moment.

Foster and Taney ran over to the ship's edge and Foster turned to Lasher with anger in his eyes. "If anything happens to one more nigger, you, Mr. Lasher, will become shark bait!"

The crew were surprised but soon went about their business. The slaves cried out, but under Lasher's watchful eye kept their mourning to themselves. Areba blinked back tears. "I did not understand the man's cry," she said to Kazoola. "What did he say?"

"He said, 'You evil White men will never have us'."

One morning in May, Nia stood on deck with Foster as he directed the crew. Five crewmen stood with large buckets, waiting for the slaves to receive their periodic washing with seawater. It was a rousing task, an entertaining event for the crew as they watched the saltwater burn the eyes and skin of the slaves. The female slaves approached, and Nia found her sister among the crowd. She watched with empathy as Areba covered her breasts and private area as the water splash upon her.

"Oh never mind that, Nia. Just cleaning off smell. Why the tears?" Foster asked.

Nia remained silent. The women held each other's gaze. Strength flowed between them and nothing could break it.

Taney knew that now was his chance. The crew was occupied on deck, washing down the cargo. As he made his way through the dark hallway toward Areba's cabin, he saw Mr. Lasher walking toward him.

"What can I help you with, Captain Taney? All of the women are on deck," said Lasher.

Startled, Taney fumbled over his words, "Oh…yes, I was just checking to make sure all of them were on deck."

"Sir, I just told you they were all on deck," Lasher responded. He stood waiting for Taney to leave. "Is there anything else, sir?"

"No…of course not," Taney responded. He turned to go back on deck. As he walked away, regretting his lost opportunity, he heard Lasher following closely behind. Taney took his post at the prow of the ship.

The man in the crow's nest shouted, "Ship ahoy!"

Taney pulled out his spyglass and had a look. "Ship ahoy!" he echoed, alerting Foster and the rest of the crew. Taney had another look. He recognized the ship. "It's the *USS Constellation*," he informed Captain Foster. "She's an elite ship, commissioned to fight the slave trade. She's much larger than most other ships trying to stop us, and can carry a heavier battery of guns."

"Don't worry, we have someone looking out for us. We paid good money to make sure nothing goes wrong. They shouldn't take chase," said Taney.

"I am still going to take precaution anyway," said Captain Foster. He immediately ordered one of the crewmen to lower the United States flag and raise the Spanish flag in its place to avoid detection. "And take these slaves below deck!"

The diversion was handled too late—the *Constellation* had spotted the *Clotilda* and gave chase.

"I thought you said they wouldn't take chase! Damn you, Taney! Hoist all sails!" Foster ordered.

The *Clotilda* attempted to outrun the bigger ship. All hands were on deck, working feverishly to move the ship through the choppy seas with utmost speed.

Captain Foster gripped the rails, never taking his eyes from the approaching ship. Not only was his money at stake, but now his reputation as well. Despite giving it everything the ship had, the *Constellation* closed in on the *Clotilda* and fired a shot across her bows. Taney and most of the crewmen had never fought a day in their lives. The boom of the cannon terrified them and they dove for cover.

"All hands on deck, you chicken bastards, and take your places!" Foster ordered. One by one they crept from their hiding places.

In the blink of an eye, a strong crosswind caught the *Clotilda*'s sails and whisked her away. As night fell, the *Clotilda* had given the *Constellation* the slip.

"I told you not to worry," Taney said smugly.

Foster looked at Taney with a sneer and walked away.

Three days passed. The sea was calm and the wind blew at a slow five knots. The ship drifted at a slow pace. The sun beat down and the crew were exhausted. They were ready to throw Chef James overboard if he served them one more meal of salt pork and hard tack. Worse, water was running low.

In the hold, conditions were beyond abysmal. One slave after another fell ill. Those who had not yet succumbed could do nothing but endure. Among the crew, those who had fallen ill could at least be separated from the ones expected to work.

Foster saw the calamity and was troubled. He could not afford to lose any of his crew or more slaves. His pay would be tremendously affected by the demise of each slave. And there were only just enough men to handle the ship and the upkeep of her cargo.

Foster went below to assess the cargo. Men and women were packed together, heaving and sweating. Some appeared to be nearly dead.

In his frustration, Foster looked to Nia for help. The knots forming in his stomach began to ease as soon as he saw her. Being constantly in his cabin, Nia remained healthy and strong.

"What is troubling you, sir?" she asked.

Foster knelt and placed his head on Nia's lap. "Everyone is ill. The doctor himself is incapacitated with fever. I am afraid they will all die if something isn't done soon. What should I do, Nia?"

Nia stroked Foster's head. "Sir, the situation is very bad. I will need a little time, but I will try to help," she replied.

Foster nodded and stood. "I thank God for you, Nia,"

he murmured, touching her cheek. "Now I must go. I must speak with Taney."

When he had gone, Nia peered through the window in the cabin door. Several sick slaves were being taken to the deck. She recognized that they had high fevers, so common in these conditions that the men called it ship fever. It would be a challenge for the medicine man to treat so many at one time.

As soon as they passed, she slipped out of Foster's room and made her way to the cabin where Areba was kept.

"Sister!" Nia whispered loudly.

"Nia!" Areba's heart leapt with joy when she saw her sister through the round window in the door that separated them. "How did you get out?" she asked.

"Foster forgot to lock the door today," Nia responded. "He is very upset by the sickness."

"My beautiful sister Nia, I have some sad news for you. When the Dahomey captured us for these horrible White men, I fear that our parents were killed." She lowered her head in grief. "I did not see what happened to them, but many in our village died."

Nia began to cry. "Oh, Areba. Our family has grown too small. You are more precious to me now than ever." She took a deep breath. "I must get back. He wants me to tell him how to get rid of this illness that has taken over the ship. What do I do, dear sister?"

"The medicine man from our village is down below with the others. He is your answer. Tell Foster how the medicine man healed our village. Tell him that he must trust the medicine man's ability to do miracles."

Nia nodded her thanks and turned to go.

"Nia, wait. The stones. Do you still have the stones?" Areba asked.

"Yes. I am never without them," Nia responded. The sisters smiled at each other. Nia hurried back to her cabin.

She barely had time to close the door behind her and cross the room before Foster burst in. "Do you have an answer for me?" he asked.

Startled, Nia responded with a slightly shaky voice. "Yes, sir. The ship's doctor will not recover from his illness. There is a medicine man among the slaves. You must treat him well and keep him strong, and he will care for everyone onboard. He once healed our entire village of fevers."

Without a word, Foster turned on his heel and left the room. Lasher approached him. "Captain Foster, sir. The doctor has died."

Foster paused for a moment, then paced the floor thinking about the most honorable way to dispose of the doctor's body. He turned to Lasher. "We have no other choice but to toss him overboard. We'll send a message to his family when we arrive home. Take care of it," Foster said regretfully. "when you finish take Nia down below to translate and tell the one who is called the medicine man to get up here right away."

The medicine man came to Foster wearing metal shackles. His stench hit Foster like a wall. "Clean this man," he ordered. "Unchain him and feed him at once! We must keep him strong. He is our last hope for the survival of this crew and the slaves we carry."

After the medicine man had been cleaned and fed, Nia was summoned to translate for him. Foster led them to where the sick crew lay. "Tell him to help them," he urged Nia. Nia spoke softly to the old man and he nodded.

The medicine man felt foreheads, necks, wrists, and stomachs. He pulled open eyes and placed his ear on chests. Most of the men were too weak to object to being handled by a slave.

The medicine man turned to Nia. "These men have a high fever, but I can make them well again." He held up one of the pouches at his side. "I need to steep these herbs in a large pot of water."

Nia translated this to Foster and he nodded to a crewmen. "Get the medicine man whatever he needs. I'll stay with these men."

The crewman led the pair to the galley. Before Chef James could protest, the crewman ordered him to leave. "Out! Captain's orders."

Nia immediately set to boiling a pot of water. The medicine man took the pouches from his side and laid them out on the table. He removed some herbs, bark, and powders of crushed roots. When the water was ready, everything went into the pot.

Nia watched as the medicine man stirred the pot. He began to chant as fragrant steam rose. She recognized the words, and felt her heart open to the sounds and smells of her tribe's way of healing. When he had finished, he asked Nia to tell the crewman to carry the pot back to the sick crew. Foster made way for them and stood nearby watching. The medicine man dipped a cup into the mixture and held it to the lips of each sick man. After every man had drunk a small portion, he redipped the cup and held it out to Foster. Foster recoiled and looked to Nia. "He says that everyone needs to drink some, sir. It will keep the sickness from spreading." Foster hesitated. Finally, he reached for the cup and tilted some into his mouth. "Now you," he said to Nia, handing her the cup. Nia took a sip and cringed at the bitter taste.

The crew walked throughout the entire ship with pot and cup. After they confirmed that every crewmen and slave had taken the mixture, the medicine man turned to Foster and said in his language, "Give it some time. They will recover."

The weather was very hot throughout the evening, but the seas remained calm and the ship continued on its path to Mobile.

The sun rose slowly on the horizon. "Captain Foster! Captain Foster!" Screams rang through the ship. Taney banged on Foster's cabin door. Foster dragged himself from the cot and opened the door.

"What in hell is the ruckus about, Taney?"

"Sir, all of the crewmen and slaves are healed. They are as well and strong as if nothing ever happened." Relief flooded Foster's face and Taney grinned. "That old medicine man is really something," Taney admitted. Foster closed the cabin door and turned to smile at Nia.

CHAPTER NINE

It was late afternoon on a Sunday when the *Clotilda* drew close to Mobile. Foster ordered Mr. Lasher to keep the slaves below deck so they would be hidden. Areba was also ordered to join the other slaves. Foster planned to unload the slaves in the late evening, using the cover of darkness. He anxiously looked toward the harbor. Several ships were near the shore, and a tugboat was approaching the *Clotilda*.

"Hello, boys!" Foster yelled to three young men with familiar faces in the small boat below. "Where is Meaher?"

"He is back at the plantation," one of the young men yelled looking up at Foster. "You are a few days early, so he did not expect you. We sent someone to get him when we saw you from afar. It's all over town about you bringing slaves to Mobile. The federal authorities knew that you were coming, but they too are expecting you in a couple of days."

"That's precisely why we are early," Foster said with a grin. "Tell Meaher I will meet him at the bayou next to Spanish River at dusk." Foster ordered the ship to turn along the coast.

Timothy Meaher's plantation was in Plateau, near the Mobile River just outside of Mobile. His home was situated on a five hundred-acre plantation. Two sawmills sat in the piney woods at the left of Meaher's house.

Meaher sat on his large front porch, breathing in the fragrance of the Magnolia trees and roses that grew in the front of the grand white home. He sat in his favorite rocking chair, wearing his Sunday best pinstriped suit and waiting for his wife and two young daughters to finish dressing for afternoon church service.

Several months had passed since Foster and Taney had departed, and he knew that if the venture was successful Foster should return with the goods soon. Meaher worried about the rumors he'd heard in town. He knew that the authorities were watching him.

Mrs. Meaher opened the screen door, well-dressed with her handbag over her arm. She stepped outside onto the porch and caught sight of a man riding his horse along the highroad through the swamp to the Meahers' property.

"Who is that coming up the road? Seems that he is in a rush."

Meaher turned to see the rider. "It looks like Ben Collins." Meaher watched the horse and rider approach, waiting at the bottom of the steps to greet his friend. Ben stepped down from his horse.

"So what brings you here, Ben?"

Ben paused and looked at Mrs. Meaher. "Honey, go inside; I need to speak with Mr. Collins for a moment."

When she had disappeared inside, Ben spoke up.

"Captain, Foster and Taney have arrived. But I didn't see any niggers!"

"What! You were in charge of the sentinels who were supposed to be on the lookout for Foster and Taney's arrival. Why didn't I know sooner?" Meaher yelled. He didn't wait for an answer. "Wait here! I must change clothes." Meaher soon returned and headed toward the stables.

"Foster said for you to meet him at the bayou next to Spanish River at dusk," Ben told him. Meaher nodded. They mounted their horses and headed out, stopping by the slave quarters to pick up Meaher's overseer, Cyrus.

Cyrus was a muscular Black man who wore a scar across his face and stood taller than six feet.

"Cyrus knows many tribal languages, and I expect his skill will be useful," Meaher told Ben. Meaher summoned Cyrus, who mounted a horse and rode alongside his master, listening.

"Do you have the three tugboats ready?" asked Meaher.

"Yes, three of my fastest boats are ready, Captain. I knew you would need to move everyone from the ship as quickly as possible," Ben replied.

"Well done."

After their hour-long ride, the men arrived at the docks to the three boats awaiting them. Several men were waiting to assist Meaher. They loaded the boats with ropes, chains, and saddlebags. When they had finished, the boats quickly pulled away from shore and headed up the river to meet the *Clotilda*.

Foster and the crew waited impatiently for Meaher. Fearful of being spotted, Foster glided slowly along the shoreline. Just before sunset Foster guided the *Clotilda* into the bayou. As the ship crept along the shoreline, Foster saw Meaher waiting with the tugboats. When the tugboats approached, Taney threw over a rope ladder over the side and Meaher climbed up to the ship's deck with Cyrus following closely behind.

"Welcome back, gentlemen. You made good time," Meaher said. He shook Foster's hand and then Taney's.

"We did, sir," Foster said. "Shall I show you the goods?"

"Of course," Meaher answered.

Foster nodded to a member of the crew, who went below. "I also have wonderful news for you, Captain," he said.

"What could be better than you arriving with these slaves and us winning the bet?" Meaher asked.

The crewman returned with a slave woman. "This is your surprise, Captain!" Foster said as he grabbed Areba's arm and put her in front of Meaher. "This one is especially for you, Captain, and she is quite special. She speaks very good English and seems to be a leader to the others. There is something very different about her."

"But if you don't want her," Taney broke in, "I'll take her, Captain." He had hoped Foster had forgotten about giving her to Meaher.

Meaher grinned. "I'm touched, Foster, thank you. Sorry, Taney. I'll be keeping this one." Taney shrugged, trying not to show his disappointment. "So, how many niggers survived the voyage?" Meaher asked.

"All but seven," Foster replied.

"Seven!"

"Illness filled the ship, Captain, and some died. Not a bad number, really," Taney replied, leaving out the beatings of women and men thrown overboard.

Foster glanced at Taney and quickly turned to Mr. Lasher and the crew. "Bring up the niggers!" Foster ordered.

The crew began unchaining groups from the walls and sending them up the stairs. Lasher stood over the hull with his whip ready to discipline anyone who gave them trouble.

Meaher looked them over carefully. "They are not as healthy as I would have hoped, Foster."

"The fevers hit us hard, the crew too, and we lost the doctor. All things considered, I'd say they're in pretty good condition," Foster answered defensively.

Meaher waved his hand. "Never mind. Take the slaves in the tugboats and hide them in the marsh north of the bay until morning. We will split up the slaves early tomorrow.

"Now you must take anything of value left on the *Clotilda*. When it's done, I want her burned to the hull," said Meaher. "Cyrus and I will go inform all potential buyers of tomorrow morning's meeting time and place."

"I'll take care of it, Captain," said Foster.

Foster, Taney, and the crew began unloading the slaves. The darkness did not make it easy, and more than a few nearly ended up in the water. Nia and Areba were put in one of the tugboats with Foster and Billy. The sisters' clasped hands were hidden from view by Nia's skirts. Billy watched Areba with admiration. Although he'd hardly caught sight of her during the journey, she seemed to be strong and wise, and a leader. He'd never forget the way she stood up to Foster. Their tugboat headed for the marsh along with the second one. The third, intended for the crew, and stayed behind.

When the crew had finished clearing the ship, Taney and two other crewmen tossed kerosene lanterns onto the *Clotilda*'s deck. The men ran for the ladder and took their places on the tugboat. As the tugboat pulled away, Taney watched the flames light up the night.

Captain Foster, Taney, Lasher, Billy, and the crew were to keep watch over the slaves that night. Everyone was ready to be on solid ground again, and a night on the marsh was most unwelcome. Only Nia and Areba were grateful that the journey was not yet over because they would be separated again come morning.

Meaher and Cyrus returned to the marsh early the next morning. The slaves were prepared for trade. Slave buyers appeared at the appointed time, rushing all at once into flat land right outside the marsh where the slaves would be sold.

Meaher saw John Taylor and Paul Reed approach. "Well, well the New Yorkers actually showed up to make good on our bet," he said. He grinned at Foster. "Gentlemen, I believe the bet was that if I could bring the slaves to Mobile, you would each pay fifty thousand. Is that how you remember it, Foster?"

"Yes, sir, that was the bet," Foster replied.

"I remember what the bet was," John Taylor said steadily. He counted bills into Meaher's hand until he reached one hundred thousand dollars.

"I think that settles our bet, gentlemen. Now let's get on with the selling," Meaher said, nodding to Taylor and Reed. When the New Yorkers had departed, he turned to Foster, Taney, and the crew. "I will settle up with all of you after the sale."

Excitement filled the air as buyers began sizing up each slave and making their selections. Buyers were eager, though they knew the venture was prohibited by law. Cotton ruled, and if they had to break the law to improve production, so be it.

Within an hour, each slave was auctioned off. Relatives and friends were separated. Areba knew that, unlike she and Nia who had been reunited in America, most of these people would never to see their loved ones again. She overheard the crew talking about many of the new slaves being taken to a place called Selma, Alabama. She wondered where Mr. Meaher would be taking her and where Mr. Foster would be taking Nia.

Meaher retained thirty Africans, including Areba and Kazoola. Nia sat next to Areba waiting pensively to see what would happen next. She saw Meaher pass money to Foster. She looked away, angry. He had taken money for enslaving her people, and any affection she felt for him was tempered with hatred.

Foster went over to his group of six slaves and called to Nia. She squeezed her sister's hand, and they looked into one another's tear-filled eyes hating that they would be separated once again.

Nia leaned over and whispered in Areba's ear. "Don't worry, sister. We will be only a short distance apart, so I will find you. She stood, and went to her master.

Meaher and Taney exchanged money and Taney gathered his three female slaves.

"Foster," Meaher called. "I would like for you to take

one of my ships to drop off the crew in Montgomery and settle up with them. How about it?"

"That would be fine, sir, for a few extra dollars. But I need to take my slaves to my plantation first," Foster said.

"Mr. Lasher, take the crew down to my boat, but keep them out of sight until Foster's return," Meaher ordered.

Meaher gathered his slaves and took them back to his plantation. Cyrus followed closely behind the group with a whip in hand.

Foster, Nia, and the new slaves arrived at his plantation at noon. Foster led the group into the house and ran upstairs to quickly prepare for his next journey.

"Nia!" he yelled. She left the slaves standing in the foyer and went quickly to his bedroom where he was packing some clothing.

"Yes, sir."

"Nia, I will be away for a couple of days. If the authorities come looking for me, tell them I am away and you do not know when I will return. While I am gone, take care of the new slaves and help them settle in. Show them to their quarters, give each of them the chores I've assigned, feed them well, teach them good grooming habits, and everything else they need to know. And one last thing, if any of them do not do what they are supposed to, tell Lasher."

"Well…I…I don't know how to tell my own people to do chores, sir. It just doesn't feel right.

"Stop there, Nia. I am not asking you to do this. I am

ordering you. I will make it clear to the slaves that they need to follow your instructions and what will happen if they don't."

Foster took the crew to Meaher's ship at the docks. He prepared the ship and right before they set sail, Billy decided that he did not want to go to Montgomery.

"Sir, I've decided not to go to Montgomery. Could we settle up now?"

"I suppose," Foster said. He counted out some bills. "Here is your share for the journey."

"Sir, that is half of what you promised!"

"It's all you'll get. Now git out of here and keep quiet," Foster said. Billy snatched his money and walked away. "Get ready to sail!" Foster yelled, and he headed the ship toward Montgomery some two hundred miles away.

When they reached Montgomery Foster settled up with the crew paying them exactly what was promised. "This has been an adventure you will always remember, men. You are a part of history on the *Clotilda*." The crewmen didn't care about Foster's speech. They jumped off the ship and quickly disappeared without a word.

By the time Foster arrived back in Mobile, word had spread that Meaher and Foster had been successful in their attempt to import slaves.

The town sheriff and his men entered the homes of both men, handcuffed them, and took them to the jailhouse. Within an hour, their attorneys paid bond and they were released.

The next morning, Meaher opened the paper and grinned. Headlines stated: "Authorities investigate illegal slave ship; no evidence found." The sub headlines read, "No slave ship could be produced."

CHAPTER TEN

"Cyrus, take Areba to her new living quarters," Meaher said.

Areba walked with Cyrus across some railroad tracks about one-half mile east of Meaher's home.

"This is the African Quarters," Cyrus told her. "Your new home." There were twenty-eight cabins sitting in a semicircle. "There are eighteen of us here now," Cyrus said. "And it looks like Master Meaher done brought about thirty more of you, so we'll be full up."

Areba noticed American Negroes around the cabins. How long had they been in bondage in America? Had their parents once been part of her tribe? They had the same dark skin and high cheekbones. Areba quickly dismissed the thought because these dark people spoke perfect English like the White man, and seemed just as unfriendly. The Negroes stared at Areba, their faces betraying their disgust. She overheard them referring the newest slaves as "savages." The American Negroes clearly disapproved of Areba and all of the newly arrived Africans and would not welcome them.

Cyrus came to a stop in front of a small cabin. "Here

is your cabin, Areba. You are lucky that Mr. Meaher is allowing you to have a cabin of your own," he added. He pointed to a pump on the far side of the semicircle. "There is where you get your water. I will give you your work assignments when the sun rises tomorrow. Plan to work from sun up until sun down, six days out of the week. On Sundays, you will have some free time, but Meaher will let you know more about that.

"I live there," he added, pointing to the large house at the end of the semicircle. "If you need anything, see me." Cyrus looked her in the eye. "There are no secrets. I carry out Meaher's orders, and I report everything to him. So don't make any problems." With that, he walked away and left Areba on her own.

Areba stepped into her one-room cabin, passing a stack of wood by her door. There was one cot, a fireplace, an iron pot, a few dishes, a tin tub, and water kettle. She walked over to the mantle and took out her sacred stones. She held the stones with both hands as she prayed to see Nia once again. When she had finished, she hid the stones inside of an urn on the mantle, wrapped in a small piece of cloth and covered them with the sandy dirt from outside.

Areba was anxious to cleanse the dirt, seawater, and White man's touch from her body. She placed the tub in the center of the floor and fetched water from the well using her kettle. Then she warmed the kettle over an open fire in her fireplace, and poured the warm water into the tub. She had to repeat the process seven times to fill the tub, but finally she dipped her toe into the warm water and then slid all the way in.

Her mind drifted to Nia. She wondered if her sister was safe. Soon she drifted to sleep with her head resting on the edge of the tub, and she dreamed about Nia coming to see her with word of a war between the White men.

The next morning, Meaher ordered Cyrus to gather every slave on the front lawn. Cyrus met Areba and the new slaves at first light and walked them down the dirt road to Meaher's plantation. When they reached the house, Cyrus pointed them toward the lawn.

Areba marveled at the sight of Black and White children playing together, and was amazed to see how attached the White children seemed to be to their Black nursemaid.

Meaher stood before them now, sizing up his newest acquisitions. Areba and Kazoola stood together near the porch stairs. Meaher turned to Cyrus and told him to translate for the new slaves.

"Your heart, mind, and soul now belonged to me, Master Meaher. You will work long hours and will do as you are told. Those who do as they are told will be fed well and will have some time with their families one day per week."

Meaher walked over to Kazoola and looked dead into his eyes.

"Anyone who tries to run away from this plantation will be hunted down with dogs. When you are found, you will be dragged back and will be given twenty lashes with a whip. While you are still bleeding from the lashes on your backside, your four smaller toes will be removed and you will still be expected to work in the fields.

"If you do something I really don't like, you will receive a slow and painful death."

Not understanding Meaher's words, Kazoola stared back at him, defiant. Cyrus repeated Meaher's words in various languages. When Kazoola finally understood, his attitude quickly changed.

"You, Areba, will serve as a maid's helper. You will help with the house cleaning and taking care of my children."

After Meaher finished going over assignments, a Black servant approached Areba and smiled warmly. "Hello. My name is Maggie."

"Hello, I am Areba."

"Yo' English sho' is good," Maggie said, surprised.

"Thank you," Areba said, suddenly conscious of her thick accent and how different Maggie sounded.

Maggie nodded toward the children playing. "They have no idea 'bout this ugly slavery they were born into. When they grow older they will learn to adjust ta it just as we have. You gonna learn too, Areba," Maggie added.

"I don't think I will ever get used ta being someone's slave. It's just not right. Why didn't they just get Americans ta be their slaves…why did they have to come all the way to Africa to get us?" Areba asked.

"I cain't answer that, Areba. The only thing I can tell ya is that you must be pretty special ta be here. Mr. Meaher only chooses slaves who can fill a specific need. I've learned to clean just da way Mrs. Meaher likes, and when I make sweet pies and other desserts, dey eat em so fast I cain't remember makin' 'em. John over there is excellent with plants and harvesting. Everyone here has a special talent or gift. So what is yours?"

"Well...I...I'm not sure why he chose me. In truth, it was Captain Foster who gave me as a 'gift' to Mr. Meaher," Areba admitted uncomfortably.

"Still, he must have seen something in you he liked," Maggie said, leading Areba into the kitchen. "You are to wait on the Meaher family and their guests. Mr. Meaher wants you to do the weaving, help me with the cleaning, and care for the children. Make the children love you then his wife will love you, too, and Meaher will treat you well. The children, Joshua and Amanda, are eight and six and are quite lovable and easy to care for. I've watched them grow from brand new babies."

"How long have you been here, Maggie?"

"I was born here. My daddy was never known. I don't want to guess who it may be, but my light skin color may be a good indication," she said, holding her hand out and regarding it. "My mama died when I was just five years old and she never told me who my daddy was. So Mr. Meaher keeps me here in the house to work for him."

Suddenly Maggie straightened up and Areba turned to see a White woman standing there. "Mrs. Meaher, this is your new maid's helper and nursemaid, Areba," said Maggie.

"Hello, ma'am," Areba said bowing her head.

"Hello, Areba. I would like for you to go tend to the children. You can tell the girl out there to come in and help in the kitchen."

Areba went over to the children and sent the other servant in. She introduced herself to Joshua and Amanda and answered them patiently when they asked about her accent. Soon Amanda had taken her hand and pulled her off in one direction, wanting to show her the berries they could pick down by the river.

Areba found herself smiling as she listened to Amanda's chatter. The child ate as many berries as she picked, pausing occasionally to throw stones in the water. When Amanda's skirts became caught in the thorns of the berry bushes, Areba did her best to free the cloth without damaging it. When she straightened up, she realized that the small rowboat that she'd noticed on the bank was not there. Joshua had pushed it into the water and had taken it out alone.

"Joshua, bring that boat back over here before you end up in the sea," she called sharply.

"Don't worry. I know how to row," he assured her.

Areba watched him anxiously, knowing the current was too strong for such a small boy. "That's right, Joshua," she encouraged. "Keep coming this way." The boat hit a rock and Joshua lost his grip on an oar.

He watched, frightened, as the oar floated downstream. "I lost an oar! I can't get it! Help me!"

Mrs. Meaher and Maggie heard the panicked sound and came running.

All of a sudden, the boat flipped and Joshua disappeared in the water.

"Oh God!" cried Mrs. Meaher. "Please don't let anything happen to him!"

Before Mrs. Meaher had finished her plea, Areba had pulled off her shoes and run into the water. She reached the overturned boat and went under.

Mrs. Meaher held onto Amanda, eyes locked on the spot where Areba had disappeared. Finally, Areba broke the surface, her arm around Joshua's middle. She swam frantically to shore and pulled him to the sand with Maggie's help.

"He's not breathing!" Mrs. Meaher said hysterically. "Help him! Help!"

Areba placed her mouth over Joshua's and pumped his upper stomach. She repeated the action as Mrs. Meaher stood by holding her breath.

After what seemed an eternity, Joshua began coughing and water sputtered from his mouth. Areba raised him a bit and turned him over to help him breathe.

"Areba!" Joshua said weakly. Mrs. Meaher bent down the hugged her son. "Mother, I wanted to show her that I could row," he said.

"Shhh, darling, it's all right," she soothed. As she held him she looked over at Areba. Areba waited to be chastised, maybe punished. Instead, Mrs. Meaher reached over and grasped her hand and said, "Thank you, Areba. I do not blame you, and I will never forget what you did today."

The next day Areba stood at the well, her mind uneasy, her thoughts scattered. She felt so alone and uncertain without her family. She ached to be near Nia again. She wondered how Nia was being treated at Foster's home. She wondered how she would be treated here.

She thought of Maggie, who had lived her whole life here. How must it have been for her, growing up without a mother and not knowing her father? But maybe she did know him. Her hair and skin appeared to be half White mixed with African blood, and she'd been taken care of by Mr. Meaher since her mama died. Areba could not help but believe that Mr. Meaher himself was her father.

Areba was so grateful to Maggie. After the near disaster at the river, Maggie had given Areba dry clothes and they spent the rest of the day together. Maggie showed her how to do her work, and helped her learn Mrs. Meaher's quirks. Areba felt she would be lost without Maggie's kindness and was never more thankful for friendship.

In her first days on the plantation, Areba expected that at the end of the day, all the slaves would return to the African Quarters and catch what little sleep they could before rising again with the sun. She soon discovered that work did not end when they left the main house and fields.

The inhabitants of the African Quarters worked well into the night, for themselves and for each other. As they left the fields, fathers gathered fuel for cooking, while mothers hurried home to check on the children left in the quarters during the day and to begin meal preparations. After supper, the adults worked small garden plots with the help of the children. The young ones held pine torches so that the adults and older children could see to plant or pull weeds. Even later into the night fathers and sons, and sometimes mothers and daughters, hunted or fished for the next day's meal.

One Sunday, Areba was outside her cabin doing her washing. Many of the other women were doing the same, and she could hear them talking. Although they looked like her, they did not sound like they were from Africa. These were American Negroes, she thought, born and raised here. The Americans and Africans did not mix together. Areba looked around for the men and women from the *Clotilda*. They were working silently as she was, keeping to themselves.

Kazoola passed by with an armload of wood, and he paused to greet her. "Hello, Areba."

"Hello, Kazoola," Areba answered, grateful to hear her own language again. "It is good to speak to you. My heart aches when I see our people, so alone in this new land. We live and work with those who look like us, and yet we are different. Do you see it, too?"

"I see that the American Negroes do not try to speak to us because we do not know their language." Kazoola paused. "But you, Areba, do know the language that is spoken here. Will you teach us?"

Areba smiled. "Yes! I see that we must create a life here and be a part of this land until we can get back home."

And so Areba began holding English lessons after sundown. She passed on the skills she learned from Maggie, showing them the American ways and the American words that went along. One evening, several Africans gathered in Areba's small yard around large pots. "Before we start on soap and dye, let's review the names of the letters," she said, using a stick to make an A in the dirt. Just then, she heard footsteps approaching in the dark. Quickly, she stepped on the letter and erased it with her foot. Lasher and Mr. Meaher stepped into the circle of light made by the pine torches.

"Then the lye and pork fat are poured into a kettle," Areba said. "When the soap is ready, we can begin preparing the cloth to make dresses. Using the strong soap, wash the flour or feeds sacks several times. It takes two sacks to make a dress. After boiling the sacks, the dye is next."

"Listen carefully to the names of these plants and the colors they make. Sumac blossoms are for red, the skin of an onion makes brown, and elderberries are for blue. I'm sure all of you know the next steps. After you remove the sacks from the dye, let them dry, and cut out a pattern. At last, we can sew the pieces of cloth together, using a needle and thread. This will take a long time, but you will like the beautiful dresses when you're done," Areba said.

She looked out past the gathered women and pretended surprise. "Oh! Hello, Mr. Meaher. Is there something you need, sir?"

"I hear that you are teaching the slaves to read. Is that true?"

"No, sir. I am teaching them how to make dresses and soap so we can wash those babies of yours."

"Fine," he said. He looked around the circle. "You all know what happens if you're caught doing something you're not supposed to do!" Meaher and Lasher walked away.

Those in the circle glanced at each other and exhaled. Areba took up her stick and made a new shape in the dirt. "Can anyone tell me the sound this letter makes?"

Gradually, the newcomers' language skills and confidence grew. The American Negroes noticed their efforts, though some were more accepting than others. By degrees, their isolation lessened and their sense of belonging grew.

CHAPTER ELEVEN

As months passed, Mrs. Meaher took a special interest in Areba. Areba had fashioned blankets for the children from pieces of cotton cloth. So impressed by Areba's skill with a needle and thread was Mrs. Meaher, that she purchased more and more cloth, and Areba made clothing for the children as well. On one occasion, Areba surprised Mrs. Meaher with a beautiful satin dress, finer than her Sunday best.

One day, Areba was cleaning the room of one of the children when Mrs. Meaher walked in.

"Good morning, Areba. That is really a pretty dress. When did you make that one?"

"Just last night, ma'am," Areba answered, standing up straight. "Oh how beautiful your dress is as well, Mrs. Meaher," she added, admiring the dress of bright green cloth. She wished she could achieve such a color in her own dyeing. "One day I hope to make a dress as pretty as yours," said Areba with a smile as she folded clothing over the bed.

Mrs. Meaher regarded Areba for a moment, and then grabbed her by the hand, leading her down the hall to a large guest bedroom. "Areba, I am going to show you how to make yourself extremely beautiful, but you cannot share this with anyone."

"I will do as you wish, Mrs. Meaher."

"Now, let me spray a bit of perfume on you." She spritzed Areba, who recognized the scent. It was the same scent she always noticed when her mistress came into a room. Next Mrs. Meaher held up one of her own older dresses. It was a lovely blue. "Now put this dress on. We're just about the same size," said Mrs. Meaher.

Areba took a step backwards. "Oh I couldn't, Mrs. Meaher."

"Yes you can, and yes you will," she answered playfully, picking up a corset and putting it around Areba. When the corset was fastened, she helped Areba into the dress. "Don't you look pretty," she said, standing back. "Turn around and look," Mrs. Meaher prompted as she turned Areba toward an oval mirror.

Areba looked in the mirror and felt confused. She saw Mrs. Meaher in front of her, even though she still stood behind her. The other woman she saw before her was a stranger. She reached out to touch the woman in Mrs. Meaher's dress, but her fingers touched a piece of glass. The woman in the glass reached out, too.

"Is that me?"

"It's you, Areba. I know this must be the first time you've ever seen yourself. You are beautiful in your new dress, just as I knew you would be."

"Are you giving this dress to me?" Areba asked her eyes widening.

"I see how wonderful you are with my children, Areba. You watch over them with pride and treat them very well. I have also noticed how the children help you to improve your English and writing when they think no one is looking."

Areba turned quickly to Mrs. Meaher. "It's not their fault, ma'am. It is all my fault, and I am sorry. Please don't be mad, Mrs. Meaher. I only want to learn," Areba begged.

"Mad! Of course I'm not. I am very pleased with them and with you. Your…extra activities will be our little secret," Mrs. Meaher assured her gently. "You have been so good to my family. You saved my child's life! My children love you and…so do I."

"Oh my!" Areba said, tears flowing from her eyes. "You know, I hated every White person in this world when they took us away from our land and did so many evil things to our people. I did not realize there were nice White people in this world. But you are good, Mrs. Meaher. You are a good wife and mother and you treat everyone very well." The two women embraced. Areba held her dress outward and turned around two times smiling and laughing. "I've never worn a dress bought from a store before," she said. Other than the sacred stones the dress was her most cherished possession.

Weeks later, Areba awoke before dawn. She still thought about her dress. It was a secret source of happiness for her. She was too afraid to wear it around the other slaves because they might believe that she had stolen it from Mrs. Meaher. Even worse, they might feel that she was favored over all other slaves.

Areba knew she was better off than most of the other Negroes, working as she did inside the house instead of out in the fields. It was true that Mrs. Meaher favored her, but she was still not sure why. Perhaps the sacred stones were keeping her safe.

She dressed and took the urn from the mantle, pulling the piece of cloth out of the sand. The sacred stones took their place in her headscarf and she began her day.

Areba arrived at the main house and immediately went to the children's rooms to check on them. She collected their dirty laundry and took it outside where she was to begin the washing.

Areba looked up and sucked in her breath. Lasher, Foster's slave driver, was walking across the lawn. She had not seen the man since arriving at the plantation.

Meaher came to greet him and they walked past Areba to walk out to the fields.

Areba reached up to her head and rubbed the stones to calm her nerves. She stared at Lasher's back, the image of him attacking her husband playing over and over in her mind. Then she saw Lasher attacking her. She didn't know when or where, but she was sure that her vision would come to fruition.

"Maggie!" she called.

Maggie appeared in the doorway. "Yes?"

"The children will be up soon. Will you please keep an eye on them while I get the water for washing?" Areba asked.

Maggie nodded. "I will go upstairs now." Maggie

climbed the stairs and headed toward the children's rooms. After peeking in on them, she went to the kitchen to start breakfast.

Mrs. Meaher stopped her in the hallway. "Where is Areba?"

Areba went to the barn to fetch the water buckets. Leaving the door ajar for light, she looked around. The door squeaked and light flooded in. Areba turned to see a man standing in the doorway.

"Hello, Areba. Remember me?" Lasher asked.

"I remember you," she said, mindful of her vision from a moment ago. "What do you want?"

"I am looking for Jonas, one of Foster's slaves. You wouldn't happen to know where he is, would you?" Lasher asked.

"If I knew where he was, I would not tell you," Areba told him.

Lasher reached out and backhanded her. "Stop sassing me, you nigger women."

Areba fell backward onto a pile of hay. Lasher lunged toward her. She tried to roll away from him, but he straddled her, pinning her down.

"I know you think you can get back at me for killing your ole man in Africa," he growled, one hand fumbling with her dress, "but you won't ever have power over me. I always have what I desire, and what I want now is your Black skin."

Lasher's hand moved to his belt. Areba pushed against his chest with all her might and brought her knee up into his groin. He groaned and lost his grip, and Areba struggled away from him and got to her hands and knees. Before she could move far enough away, Lashed grabbed her ankle and pulled her back down into the hay.

Areba screamed and fought him. Couldn't anyone hear her? She looked toward the door and saw little Amanda peeking into the barn. When Areba's eyes met Amanda's, the girl turned and ran away.

"Help!" Areba yelled. She threw hay into his face and kicked him, yet he was relentless. He increased his efforts and struggled to hold both of her wrists together above her head. Areba continued to scream and kick as his free hand reached under her dress. Suddenly, Mrs. Meaher appeared in the doorway. Lasher did not notice her, but Areba saw her wild expression, and the rifle she carried in both hands.

"Get off of her, you animal!" she yelled.

Caught, Lasher struggled to his feet and wheeled around. Mrs. Meaher, afraid for her own safety, reacted quickly. A shot rang out. Lasher's body was flung backward onto the hay within inches of Areba. He lay still.

Mrs. Meaher reached out for Areba's hand and pulled her onto her feet. "Areba, are you okay?"

Areba straightened her clothing and blotted the tears on her cheeks. "Yes ma'am, I'm okay," she replied shakily.

"Take a moment to collect yourself," Mrs. Meaher said. "Then go get Cyrus and Kazoola to gather this piece of trash so we can dispose of him before anyone comes looking."

CHAPTER TWELVE

The next day Areba tossed a ball with the children on the front lawn. Looking toward the road, she could see a wagon coming. She ran to the Meahers' front door.

"Mr. Meaher, a visitor is coming down the road!" Areba announced.

Meaher came to the porch and had a look. Foster's wagon approached, and a second wagon had appeared as well. Meaher walked out to the end of the lawn to greet Foster. Foster's horses had barely come to a stop when Taney pulled up closely behind.

Areba paid no attention to the second wagon. Nia sat in the wagon next to Foster. Areba could barely contain the joy she felt. She had not seen her sister for several months.

Nia's eyes widened when she caught sight of her sister standing in the yard, but she was careful not to draw attention to herself. She stepped down from the wagon and stood next to Foster.

Taney hitched his horses and went to greet Meaher and Foster. His eyes fixed on Nia and Areba, but he, too, gave nothing away.

"How are you doing, gentlemen?" Meaher asked.

"I'm doing well. It sure is hot and muggy today. Feels a lot like Africa," Foster said removing his hat.

"I am doing quite well myself," said Taney.

"This visit is quite a surprise. What brings you both here today?" Meaher asked as he led them to a set of chairs on the porch.

"It seems that we are all facing some problems here," Taney said. "But I think we should talk about this in private." Taney looked at Areba and Nia standing behind Meaher and Foster. He turned his chair to face Foster so he could get a good look at Nia. He looked her over carefully, wondering if the diamonds were in her clothing.

"Oh," Meaher said. "Areba, go fetch us some lemonade. Foster, your girl can go with her."

"Oh no, Foster likes to keep this one close," Taney said with a smirk.

Meaher shrugged. "You're the one who asked for privacy, Taney. She stays, then?"

"Nia is fine right here with me," Foster said. "Now, I assume you're here to discuss the political climate in the North. The abolitionists are certainly making their voices heard."

"They don't know what it's like down here with all this cotton growin' and niggers everywhere," Meaher complained. "They're not looking out for the South's interests. We're better off as our own new nation, even if we have to fight these tyrants like our forefathers did the British."

"Well, if Lincoln is elected president, South Carolina is looking to secede from the Union," said Taney.

"If Alabama secedes, we will be able to make our own decisions," Foster interrupted.

"I hope we break away from them Northerners. We would be much better off. If Lincoln is elected the South won't stand for it," said Meaher.

"That's right," said Foster. "We hanged John Brown for treason and we'll fight anyone else who tries to turn our slaves against us."

Areba returned with three tall glasses of lemonade. Each man took a glass.

"Areba, could you also get the gentlemen some cold water from the well out back," Meaher said.

Foster glanced at Nia. "Nia, go and help Areba," he said.

Nia looked at him, startled. Why would he let her go with Areba? Did he know? Before he could change his mind, she followed her sister toward the well at the back of the house.

Taney watched them go. "Excuse me, gentlemen. I forgot my pipe and tobacco in my saddlebag," he said.

Taney rounded the side of the house and kept himself hidden from the sisters as he listened.

"Nia, sister, I've missed you so much. Is Foster treating you well?" Areba asked.

"Oh yes, Master Foster cares for me a great deal." Nia smiled. "Once I believe he tried to confess his love. He protects me and would never let anything happen to me. Do not worry about me. He is just a little upset these days because Mr. Lasher never returned home after looking for a missing slave."

"Sister, Lasher killed my husband in Africa. Foster will never see Lasher again," Areba said.

Nia understood immediately. They did not dwell on Lasher a moment longer.

"Tell me about you, sister. How are those people treating you?" Nia asked.

"I am treated well here. Mrs. Meaher is a good person. She has a heart and doesn't let anyone mistreat me. She even gave me a dress! It's the most beautiful dress I have ever had."

"I know that I am a slave, but I don't always feel like one. But when I see the way the others are treated, I pray to my sacred stones that our people will be free soon. Tell me your sacred stones are still with you, Nia."

Taney held his breath as he waited for the answer.

"Oh yes, I still have them."

Taney waited to see if the sisters would reveal where they hid their stones, but they did not.

"Nia!" Foster's voice rang in the air.

"I better get back to Master Foster now," Nia said. "But I will sneak away tomorrow and meet you, now that I know the way. I could hardly contain my joy when I realized Foster was bringing me to you. The distance is not too far, and I can go through the woods."

"Kazoola, a man from our village, made a drum," Areba told her. "Wait by the large magnolia tree with the broken branch and you will hear a Yoruba drumbeat. When you hear it, you will know it is safe to come. I will put a white cloth on my doorknob so you know which cabin is mine."

After hearing this, Taney went to retrieve his pipe and tobacco.

The next morning, Nia found it difficult to concentrate on her work. All she could think about was sneaking away to see Areba that night. She was uneasy because she had seen kitchen slaves whipped for leaving the grounds. Even though she knew that Foster was very fond of her, she did not trust that he would be easy on her if she left the house. But her fears did not overwhelm her desire to see her sister. She would go to the magnolia tree to hear Kazoola's drum signal after the sun went down.

Nia forced her hands to continue working while she thought of ways to escape under Foster's watchful eye. By the time Foster had finished his supper, Nia knew what to do. Clearing his dishes from the dining table, she asked, "Master Foster, would you like your whiskey in the study?"

Foster agreed, as she knew he would. Once he'd settled into his favorite chair, she gave him two strong drinks of whiskey and kept a conversation going to measure his awareness.

"Mr. Foster, I've been thinking about what happened on the ship," Nia said carefully.

"Oh never mind that, Nia," Foster responded not meeting her eyes.

"But sir, it sounded like you were going to tell me something very important," Nia insisted.

"Important?" Foster downed his drink in one gulp.

Nia immediately refilled his glass. "I remember you had started to tell me something about how you felt... about me."

Foster drank the whiskey in one gulp once again. The whiskey soon made its effect known, and Foster stumbled over his words. "There is nothing important about how I feel about anything."

Nia poured him one last warm brandy. Foster slipped

in and out of consciousness and Nia gently took the glass before it slipped from his fingers. "Is there anything else before I go to bed, sir?"

"No," Foster grumbled, nearly falling out of his chair.

"Good night then, sir."

Nia made her way up to her living quarters. Instead of putting on her nightdress, she slipped into a coat. Taking up the lantern next to her bed, she opened the window. Carefully, she stepped over the sill and felt her toes grip the trellis below her window. As she began her descent, she heard a crack in the darkness. Nia started, nearly losing her grip on the lantern. She peered over her shoulder into the night looking for the source of the noise. Had Master Foster roused himself and discovered her missing? Seeing nothing, she continued climbing downward. Once her feet touched the ground, she walked into the darkness. Any fear she felt was outweighed by the thought of her sister waiting for her.

There she is! Taney thought. He had been waiting for her since sundown. In his eagerness, he'd almost given himself away at the start. Now he tried to maintain a safe distance, keeping his eyes on the glow of her lantern in the darkness. *When I get my hands on her, I will rip every stitch off of her until I find those diamonds.* A twig snapped beneath Taney's foot, and he froze as Nia stopped and looked around. When she continued walking, Taney decided he should catch up to her now, before they were any closer to Meaher's plantation.

Just as he'd made up his mind to catch her, Nia quickened her pace through the woods moving at a fast run. Taney grunted with effort, trying to keep up. Soon he lost sight of her lantern and was left to find his way in the dark.

Nia found the large magnolia tree and knew she had reached Meaher's land. She set the lantern down and took deep breaths, waiting to hear the Yoruba drum beat. Soon the familiar rhythm called to her, and she knew it was safe to continue to Areba's cabin.

When Taney finally approached the slave quarters, Nia had already disappeared into Areba's cabin. He peered across the way and saw a large Black man sitting outside a cabin carving a piece of wood and smoking a pipe. A shotgun stood beside him. Taney made his way around the back of the semicircle of cabins, peering into each small window to look for the sisters. Finally, he caught sight of them. They were sitting on a cot and grasping each other's hands. He ducked out of sight, his heart pounding, though from excitement or exertion he could not tell. He tried to quiet his breathing in an effort to hear their conversation. The sisters kept their voices low.

"Don't worry, sister, even if you were followed," Areba said. "Cyrus keeps watch at night. If someone is lurking, he'll take care of them." She held out a dish. "I made some sweet bread. Try a piece."

"Oh, that is good. It tastes just like Mama's."

"That is what I hoped. I've been thinking about home a lot. What bothers me more than anything is that I don't know what happened to Mama and Papa after the Dahomey invaded our village. We must get home, Nia. I've been thinking about how we can do it."

"Do you really think there is a way?" Nia asked with excitement.

"Yes, I think so. I've been listening to the White men talk when I work, and I'm learning about America. Do you know why our people are out in the White men's fields from sunup to sundown? *Cotton* is the reason we are here, Nia. The South grows cotton, not just for this country, but to sell to other countries, too. I heard Master Meaher telling another man that American cotton supplies mills in England. Cotton from Mobile is being sent to Mississippi and then to England quite often," said Areba.

"Why are you telling me this, Areba?"

"All we have to do is to hide on one of Meaher or Foster's boats that go to Mississippi, and then we can hide on the ship to England. Ships sail from England to Africa all the time."

"Ahh, do you really believe we can do it, Areba? You know that if we get caught they will hang us," said Nia.

"Nia, I would rather be dead than never find out for certain what happened to Mama and Papa," Areba vowed full of emotion.

Taney stood outside the window, listening. He thought about blackmailing the women, but what proof did he have that they were planning to run away? He knew that Foster and Meaher were extremely fond of Areba and Nia and he would have a difficult time convincing them of the plan.

"All right," Nia said. "If we do this, we will need food and water to survive. Where do we get it?"

"Mrs. Meaher gives me plenty, and I am sure you can put some aside. We will let the sacred stones guide us. You do keep them with you always, don't you?" Areba asked.

"The pouch I had for them has a hole, and I need to find a scrap of cloth and sew a new one. I do not have the stones with me now, but they are safe," Nia replied.

Taney couldn't believe his luck. *She must have hidden them somewhere in her sleeping quarters*, he thought. He crept away from the cabins and went back the way he had come, wondering how much time he had before Nia left her sister and returned to Foster's.

Moonlight was Taney's guide as he approached Foster's plantation. Returning to where he'd stood when Nia had climbed out of the top floor window, he searched the house for movement. All seemed quiet, so he crept to the trellis under Nia's window.

He climbed until he reached the window, praying the trellis would hold him. He pushed the window open and squeezed through, nearly becoming stuck. When he'd made it through and righted himself, he began fumbling around in the dim moonlight. He started with her skirts, ripping them apart looking for hidden pockets. When his search revealed nothing, he moved on to a small box in the corner. Again, he came up empty-handed. "Dammit!" he breathed. "Where are they hiding?"

The only place left to search was around the cot. Taney crawled over to it and swept his hands along the floor, reaching under it as far as he could. His fingers brushed a pair of shoes, and he pulled them out. One shoe was stuffed with cloth, and he dug into it. Immediately, his fingers hit something hard.

Before he could unwrap his treasure, he heard a noise at the window. Turning, he saw Nia climbing over the sill, a lantern in one hand. Without thinking, he ran quickly to the window and tried to push her out. Still holding the glowing lantern, Nia screamed, and gripped the window frame with her free hand, fighting her way into the room.

Once she'd gained her footing, she swung with all her strength, striking Taney in the head with the lantern. The swift swing blew out the flame. Taney stumbled and fell, dropping the stones. He searched frantically for the bundle, ignoring Nia's screams.

All of a sudden the door burst open and a dark figure filled the doorway. "Master!" Nia ran over to Foster, who stood in his nightclothes, rifle in hand. "There is a stranger in the room!"

Without hesitating, Foster raised his rifle and shot the intruder. Nia crossed the room to light a candle, her hands shaking. As she lit the candle, she heard Taney struggling for air.

"Diamonds! The diamonds!" he choked out.

"What did he say?" Foster took the candle from Nia and crouched over the wounded man. "Taney! What the hell are you doing here?" Taney lay still. "Nia, I believe I've killed him. Are you all right?"

"Yes, sir."

"What did he say, Nia?"

"I'm not sure, sir," Nia responded.

"What was he doing here? Was he trying to hurt you?"

Nia shook her head. "I don't know why he was here. I was outside taking in the night air. You had told me it was all right after dinner, if you remember." Foster nodded, not wanting to admit that he did not. "He was here when I came in, but I did not know it was Taney."

Foster sighed and held out his hand toward Nia. "I told you I would never let anything happen you. "Nia took his hand and he drew her close to him, wrapping his arm around her. After a moment, he stepped away from her. "Call the new slave driver and then wait for me in my study," he instructed. "I will take care of this."

"Yes, sir." Nia walked toward the stairs until she saw Foster go into his room, then she tiptoed back into her room and rescued the sacred stones from Taney's cold hands.

CHAPTER THIRTEEN

The next morning as Areba prepared breakfast for the Meahers in the large kitchen, she heard snapping sounds and bloodcurdling yells coming from the fields. She dropped her spoon and immediately felt her headdress for the sacred stones as she recognized the sounds were from a slave being tortured and whipped.

Maggie looked up from the pot she was scrubbing. "Kazoola got caught comin' home late last night. You better watch it, girl, wit all that schoolin' or you might git the same."

Areba could hear every crack of the whip, and every groan and cry of her poor friend. Cold chills ran over her and she wept aloud. She prayed to the stones to make it stop. Finally, the popping sound ceased and so did the cries. She knew that the pain had been too much for him to bear and that he was either passed out or dead.

Areba found no consolation in her work or in her tears. She had heard horror stories from other slaves about the White man's brutality, but this was the first time their cruelty had been turned upon someone she called a friend.

She closed her eyes tightly and prayed to her sacred stones for the torture of her people to end. A vision came to her. Kazoola stood on a platform talking to hundreds of her people. They were cheering him, and it was clear he was a great leader. Areba embraced the moment and prayed to see it realized.

When she opened her eyes and looked out the window, she saw two slaves carrying Kazoola to the barn and laying him on top of the hay. Areba's heart swelled with gladness when she saw that he lived.

Over the next two days, Areba went to Kazoola to dress his wounds and to feed him. By the third day, Kazoola was walking again. On Sunday morning, Areba and Kazoola were drawing water from the well. Kazoola heard a familiar trumpet and rumbling sound. "Did you hear that?" He looked toward the main road. The sound came again and he yelled, "Ele! Ele!"

Areba turned too and repeated the words. Suddenly, the African slaves came from their small cabins and joined Areba and Kazoola. They walked toward the road yelling, "Ele! Ele!" They looked with amazement as five elephants walked down the road leading to downtown Mobile. There were two large ones and three smaller ones. The large ones were tearing branches off the trees and eating them as they walked while the babies ran around their mamas' legs playing and pulling at bushes and grass with their trunks.

Two wagons, each with a cage on top, followed behind the elephants. The onlookers saw two monkeys in the first cage, and in the second, colorful birds.

As the elephants and wagons headed down the road

toward town, several other Africans joined Areba and Kazoola. Then some of the American Negroes joined the crowd and began mimicking the Africans and teasing them. One yelled out,

"Look! They think that they're still in Africa!"

Just then Maggie walked up to the group. She glared at the ones laughing and turned to Areba. "The elephants are with a circus," she said.

"What is a circus?" Areba asked.

Maggie explained, "It is where White people go to see animals do tricks and men perform in silly clothes with faces painted white. They are called clowns."

Areba and Kazoola stood together watching the animals go by. They listened to the musicians who followed the animals.

"This gives me an idea, Kazoola. We should create a celebration for our people. Something that we can call our very own."

Kazoola looked at Areba with a smile. "I think that is a great idea, Areba. Let's discuss it with the others."

Meaher ushered Foster into his study. "How are you, Foster?"

"On edge, same as you I expect. Things are moving quickly now. Four more states have joined the Confederacy and President Davis."

"Yes, thank God," Meaher said, pouring drinks for them. "Union troops can't expect another victory like Virginia. Hundreds have responded to recruitment drives and signed up for service in the Confederate Army."

"I hear that some of the slaves are running away to join the Union army," Foster said. He accepted the proffered glass. "Have you lost any?"

"Not yet. I can't lose any, Foster. Not to the North, nor to our army. The fields won't plant themselves. I cannot pay Whites to do what those slaves do. It would break me."

"To my relief, only a few of my slaves wanted to leave the plantation to volunteer for the Confederacy," Foster said. "I hear they are limited almost entirely to non-military service. They are taking care of horses, cooking, and hauling supplies. Some of them are even building defense installations around Mobile Bay, so don't be surprised if we run into them."

Meaher shook his head. "I thought I saw old Joe grading roads. I reckon he thinks life is easier working for the Confederate army. What pisses me off is that there is nothing I can do to get him back."

"We must believe that the Confederacy will prevail and soon all will be set to rights."

After work hours, Areba and Kazoola met with other slaves from the *Clotilda*. Areba spoke. "I'm sure you've heard talk about the fighting between the states. You probably know that Alabama and other states around us have broken away from President Lincoln and made their own government. Some of us have left the plantations to go north and fight." Areba looked around at the people she now called family. "You may wish to do the same, or you may think that now is the time to escape and run. To pursue either course would only invite danger. I believe it is best for us to stay here, together. The Bluecoats from the North will come. We will be delivered from this hell we are in, you must believe."

The sun blazed down on the backs of the men and women picking cotton. Four years of war had left everyone wondering if it would ever end, and Kazoola led them in song to uplift their spirits. Areba, attending the Meaher children as they played on the front lawn, looked toward downtown Mobile and saw dark clouds of smoke rising into the sky.

Could this be the moment? Were the Bluecoats finally coming? She gripped her sacred stones and closed her eyes. Visions of chaos erupted in her mind. Out of the chaos she saw freedom. The children ran around her, but she no longer noticed them. She turned toward the fields where Kazoola toiled and willed him to look her way. Taking her white apron into her hands, she waved it up and down.

Kazoola looked up and saw the white cloth fluttering. In spite of the hot sun, goosebumps rose on his arms. This was the moment they had been waiting for. He immediately broke out into a different song. Those working nearest him took up the new words, their voices full of joy. The deliverance song spread through the fields and filled the air, letting each slave know that the day of freedom had come.

Cyrus knew the meaning of the songs and identified with the new spirit in the slaves. He stood in the field with his whip in hand. He didn't know whether to rejoice with them or to continue to act as overseer. He lowered the whip and let the slaves continue their song.

A little girl ran barefoot and breathless down the dirt road through the center of Mobile. Looking down at her dress as she ran, she knew that her mama would be upset with her for soiling it. She pushed the thought out of her mind as she weaved her way through the chaos, heading toward the Meaher plantation. Looking behind her, she could see the Union army approaching. Smoke made her eyes water and explosions grew louder and spurred her forward.

All around her, Mobilians were loading their wagons with their personal possessions. Young boys were running in packs, setting fire to bales of hay by the side of the road. They would much rather burn Mobile down than allow the Yankees the pleasure.

Still standing on the lawn with the Meaher children, Areba saw the little Negro girl running down the road toward her. The girl warned everyone in her path about the Yankee soldiers that were coming through town. Areba could see that the girl was frantic and walked to the edge of the lawn to meet her.

"The war is coming!" the girl said, her voice hoarse. "The war is coming to Mobile and they are burning everything down!"

Just then Meaher appeared at Areba's side. He'd heard the child's announcement and he saw the smoke in the distance. Joshua and Amanda had stopped their playing and were watching their father curiously.

"What's happening, Daddy?" Amanda asked.

"Are the Yankees here?" Joshua tried to put on a brave face.

"Yes, son," Meaher answered. "It's time I go speak to Cyrus." He turned and made his way to the cotton field to where Cyrus stood overseeing the labor.

With grief, Meaher spoke. "Cyrus, the Union army is coming to Mobile. I knew this day was coming, but didn't think it would be so soon. The troops are taking whatever goods they want from the plantations. Tell everyone to pile the cotton in the barn. Then tell them that they are free to go when and where they want." Meaher turned abruptly and walked away. His stomach felt sick. All that he had, the cotton farm and lumber mill, relied on free labor. Faced with the unthinkable, he staggered into the house and fell into his wife's arms.

"Honey, the Union army is coming. The slaves are free."

Mrs. Meaher gasped. "What will we do?" she asked anxiously. "What about the cotton? And what about the house? And Areba? Joshua and Amanda love Areba." Her voice rose. "You must do something—perhaps you can pay them to work. Please John, I need Areba. I wouldn't know how to care for these children on my own!"

Meaher turned and walked away. He went into his study, closed the door and poured himself a drink, leaving Mrs. Meaher standing in the foyer with tears running down her face.

After hearing the great news from Cyrus, the slaves began walking away from the fields. Cyrus had not told them that

Meaher wanted the cotton put into the barn. Since the slaves were now free, he refused to take any further instructions from Meaher. The slaves went directly back to African Quarters. As soon as they arrived, they heard the rumble of approaching horses and found themselves face to face with the first contingent of Union soldiers. The Africans were frightened, thinking they would be captured and sold again.

A soldier dismounted and stood before them. "Are all of you being held as slaves?" he asked.

"We were slaves, but Master Meaher let us go," said Kazoola.

Suddenly, a loud cannon boomed east of Mobile. Everyone was startled and looked in the direction of the sound. The soldier mounted his horse and held the reins as the animal danced anxiously. The soldier spoke directly to Kazoola. "Tell these people that they are no longer slaves and are free to go wherever they want to go. Tell this to all the former slaves." With that, the soldiers rode off.

Captain Foster heard the cannons in the distance. "Nia!" She appeared in the doorway. "Run down to the fields and tell the Africans that they are free."

"Do you mean free to go, sir?" Nia asked.

"Yes, free to go. I knew this was coming. Those damned Yankees, the damned Union army from the North is on their way to make sure that the slaves know that they are free people."

"That means...I am free to go also, sir?" Nia asked.

Foster turned away. "That means all of you are free to go, Nia. I suppose you will leave with the rest of them...if you want." Foster's voice broke. Nia looked at her master's bent head for a moment. Then she turned and ran out of the house to the fields.

Her excitement disappeared when she saw the overseer walking around with his whip. She walked up to him and spoke hesitantly. "Master Foster wanted you to tell the slaves that they are free. There is no more slavery." She turned to her people in the fields. "We are free!" she yelled. The slaves stopped working and looked at the overseer.

"They ain't going anywhere!" the overseer said. A broad-shouldered slave named Moses stopped his work and stepped over to where Nia stood.

"Get back to work, nigger!" the overseer barked.

"He is no longer a slave. You cannot tell him what to do any longer," Nia said evenly.

"You have never led us wrong, Ms. Nia. Are you sure about that freedom?" Moses asked.

"Oh yes. Mr. Foster said that the Union army is coming. Look in the sky." Nia pointed upward. "That smoke is from the Union army burning plantations, and they are headed this way."

"In that case, I want you to know something, Mr. Overseer," Moses said. He rose up and grabbed the overseer's whip and wrapped it around his neck, then punched his mouth so hard that he fell to the ground. "That's for whipping dem women, and for lookin' at me funny. Pick up another whip and I'll kill you dead." The overseer lay on the ground without moving.

The slaves in the field were emboldened by Moses's action. They put aside their work and came toward Nia.

"You are all free! The Yankees are coming to free us!" she yelled again. "It is true. Master Foster told me to tell you that you no longer have to stay here and are free to go."

No one was sure what to do next, and the great noises and black smoke were drawing nearer and nearer. Most slaves, now free, ran away from Foster's plantation into the nearby woods.

Nia wanted to celebrate her freedom with Areba. It was something they have longed for. As she walked along the roadside, she wondered where she would go and what she would do with her life in America since she still did not have the resources to return the Africa. She knew Areba would give her good guidance.

As Nia entered the African Quarters on Meaher's plantation, she heard loud drums and saw the freed slaves dancing, laughing, and talking in large groups. Her chest swelled with joy and tears rolled down her face. Areba turned and saw Nia walking toward her. The sisters ran toward one another and embraced, rocking from side to side. They joined the group and began dancing wildly in celebration.

When they tired, they sat down on a large log next to the well. Areba dipped a cup into the well, brought it to the top, and handed it to Nia to sip first.

"Areba, I am so happy for our people. What are you going to do now that you are free?"

"I will stay here, Nia. It is my destiny. I will help build a new place for our people. I do desire to go home, but there is nothing there for me since Mama and Papa are more than likely dead and you are here."

"I am so uncertain about what I want, Areba." Nia

handed the cup to her sister. "Foster has never made me feel like a slave and he takes really good care of me. I want to go home, but I don't see how I can. What do you think I should do?"

Areba quickly grabbed Nia's hand and the two walked to Areba's cabin. Areba cupped her stones in her hand. "Hold yours, too, Nia. We will pray for guidance for you."

Nia withdrew her stones and held them in one hand, clasping Areba's hand with the other. They closed their eyes and whispered a prayer.

"I did not see an answer. Did you?" Nia asked.

"Nia, you are to return to Foster."

"What! Why? What is my purpose for going back to a slave master?" Nia shouted.

"You said yourself you've never been treated like a slave. You will be well taken care of, and you will gain the means to return home," Areba said.

CHAPTER FOURTEEN

Foster sat in his study with his head in one hand and a full glass of liquor in the other. With all of his help gone, and his most precious possession, Nia, gone too, he didn't know what to do with himself.

Foster saw a shadow out of the corner of his eye. He looked toward the doorway and saw Nia standing there. He stood and faced her with relief and a big smile.

"I prayed you would stay with me."

Nia returned a small smile. "Mr. Foster, some things will need to change."

Most of Meaher's slaves kept to the woods as well, or hid somewhere on the plantation. They were sure of nothing, only that they were slaves no longer. For most of them, their only home had been the African Quarters. For those who had come on the *Clotilda* though, their memories of Africa were strong. They met with Areba and Kazoola to determine what they would do next.

Kazoola spoke first. "Areba and I understand that there is overwhelming consensus that you all, we all, would like to return to Africa. But we must be realistic. The journey requires money, lots of money, a boat, and a crew to start. Although we are free, the war is not over, and every man and every resource is needed for that effort. We will need to make the best of where we are, and since we are no longer slaves, we can demand to earn pay from Mr. Meaher. Over time, we can save the funds for the journey back to Africa."

"We believe this is our best choice. Is everyone with us?" Areba asked.

Most of them agreed to stay. A few decided to leave Meaher's land and look for family members or travel North to make a new life.

Meaher was in his study with a drink in hand when he heard a knock at his door. He continued to sit until he heard the knocking once more, and he remembered there were no slaves to assist him. He rose and pulled the door open.

"Areba, Kazoola, what are you doing here?" Meaher asked.

"Sir, by the looks of your home and fields you need help around here," Areba said. "The Africans are a proud people and we want to earn our living just like everyone else. We can help you, but we want to continue living in African Quarters until we can buy our own land. We want to work for pay.

"We ask that you assign each family a small tract of land to farm, provide some of our food until we can grow our own, and give us seeds and farm equipment to begin our own farms."

"Well, well Areba, they said that you were pretty smart. You sure do have all of this worked out, don't you?" Meaher said. "Well, let me think about this." He turned away and rubbed his head.

Damn, why didn't I think ahead! I have depended so greatly on slave labor, and now I don't have time to look for other options. All the men are gone. I can't believe they have the upper hand on this one. He turned back to Areba and Kazoola.

"Okay, I will hire all of you and I agree to provide you with all of the items you have requested. I will pay the lot of you. Areba and all house workers will be paid twenty dollars a month."

The Africans from the *Clotilda* raised crops and sold any surplus. By 1866, they had saved enough money to purchase land from Timothy Meaher. They worked together to build thirty small houses on one and a half square miles of swampland near Meaher's plantation. It was a poor rural area north of Mobile known as Magazine Point-Plateau, but the Africans called it African Town.

Soon Africa Town became a largely self-governing community of ex-slaves, from the *Clotilda*. One of their first major projects was the construction of a church. When that was done, they built a school and a community building. They also constructed their own market places, where they sold goods to people inside and outside of the Africa Town community.

They spoke in their native tongues, and communication

was often difficult. Kazoola's knowledge of African languages was a great help to many, and he often served as translator. He was soon elected town leader just as Areba's vision had shown her all those years ago.

Areba had a cabin of her own. It was very small, but adequate. She still spent most of her time at the Meaher house, working eighteen-hour days. When she was not working or teaching the Africans how to read and write, Areba and Nia spent time together. They cherished the freedom to spend time in one another's company. Often they discussed how they could help their people with the guidance of the sacred stones. They never forgot what their mother had told them. Those who found the stones were the chosen ones, and they embraced that responsibility.

Within the African enclave, they helped raise the children, teaching them the languages and values they had learned from their families and brought from the homelands they cherished.

Areba raised funds to help former slaves gain access to food, shelter, and education, and established a care facility for the elderly at a small vacant home in Africa Town.

One morning Areba opened a back door of the Meahers' house and tossed the dirty water from her cleaning bucket. She looked into the distance and noticed a new man working at the sawmill. She was taken aback by his strong and handsome physique, but quickly dismissed her thoughts and returned to work.

Later that afternoon, Areba was out hanging clothes.

She stood with wet bed covers in both hands trying to hang them over the rope well above her head. As she flung one side of the bed cover over the rope, she glanced up toward the roof and noticed the handsome stranger up there making repairs.

"You're all over the place aren't you?" Areba called, wishing she could get a clear view of his face. "Would you like some cold water?"

"Yes ma'am, I would love some," he replied.

Areba left and quickly returned with a cold jug of water. The stranger climbed down the ladder to meet her. Once on the ground, he turned to her with a smile.

"Billy!" Areba nearly dropped the jug as she recognized the carpenter from the *Clotilda*.

"Areba! Oh my!" The two embraced.

"Oh my, my. It is so good to see you again, Billy."

"Every day I've hoped to see you again. I've never forgotten you. After seeing what they did to your husband, I felt responsible, as if I should take care of you."

"Responsible? Oh no, it wasn't your fault."

"Of course it wasn't, but I wanted to care for you, Areba. And now that I see you again, I still do. That is, unless you are someone else's woman?"

Shyly, Areba responded, "No one else takes care of me, Billy. Just me."

Billy smiled. "I don't mean to be too forward, but you sho is a pretty woman. I never got a chance to properly introduce myself to you on the ship, but I always thought you were so pretty."

"Thank you, Billy. You were always very respectful to

me on the ship, and I appreciate it greatly." With a shy smile she handed him the jug and turned to go inside.

"Since this is the only place that I could find work as a free Black man, you will see me here every day, Miss Areba," Billy said as she walked away.

Once inside, Areba pulled the sacred stones from her gele. The vision that came to her was not what she had hoped for. Instead of a life with a man she loved, she saw herself alone. She put the stones away and pushed the vision out of her mind. Instead, she thought of Billy's smile and the way he wanted to care for her.

The next day, Areba returned to the Meaher house full of excitement at the thought of seeing Billy again. As she made Amanda's bed, she glanced out the window and caught sight of Billy working at the sawmill. Areba watched his every move, studying the way his muscles enlarged when he lifted something heavy. She giggled at her lustful thoughts and continued her work.

Later that day, Areba took Billy more cold water and a sandwich. She continued to bring him treats from the kitchen every day thereafter.

Billy and Areba's relationship blossomed into love and they married in 1870. Many former slaves attended the wedding. Even the Meaher family attended the ceremony and were excited for the pair. Mr. Meaher killed a pig for the barbeque, and Nia baked the wedding cake. Meaher's staff set a table in the large yard under the trees, and it was soon filled with food donated by the Meahers.

Everyone cheered when the happy couple jumped the broom as part of an African ritual, and Areba glowed with happiness.

Billy moved into Areba's small cabin and they began their married life. Over the next five years, Billy and Areba had five children: Abeni, Bayo, Abimbola, Minnie, and Nicky. They soon outgrew the cabin and found a dilapidated house in Africa Town with three rooms. Billy wanted better for his family, but the Meahers could no longer afford to keep him on. Billy became increasingly depressed as work became scarce throughout the South.

Billy walked up to twenty miles every day to look for work, but he found nothing. Conditions only worsened. A terrible drought had yielded a poor harvest. The price of wheat had tripled, and the prices of butter and milk had quadrupled. Salt, the only preservative available for meat, was very expensive. Families throughout Mobile were suffering, especially in light of an outbreak of yellow fever.

Billy became exceedingly restless and depressed because he could barely provide for his family. The only food their family had was what Mrs. Meaher sometimes gave to them without Mr. Meaher knowing. The scraps of bread, beans, peas, flour, and cornmeal were taken gratefully, though it hurt Billy's pride. Areba stored as much of the dry goods as she could, never knowing when more would come.

One evening after a long day of searching for work, Billy returned home tired and hungry. He opened the cabin door to noisy children and a home in disarray.

"Areba," he called out. Opening the door to their bedroom, he found Areba lying in bed very ill. He rushed over to the bedside. "Areba, what is wrong?"

"I have tried to take care of the children Billy, but I became ill yesterday and cannot get out of bed." Her voice was weak. "We have little food. There was only enough for the children and for you. There is bread and soup on the table."

Billy dropped his head into his hands and hid his face with shame. "Areba, I have tried and tried, but I cannot find work. I feel worthless to you and our children."

After a few moments, he left the room and returned with the food, sitting close to the bed to share with Areba. The children crowded around the bed, watching Billy feed Areba and hoping she would get better.

"Daddy, why are you always away from home?" Abimbola asked. "I want you to stay home with us. Will you, Daddy?"

Billy sat staring at his soup, then at his darling children and wife. He was ashamed of the man he had become. And now his wife was ill and there was nothing he could do for her. After putting the children to bed, Billy sat up all night thinking, staring at the small cabin, his children in the sleeping area near the table and at his wife through the doorway, caught by a fever and sleeping fitfully.

When the sun rose the next morning, Areba rolled over and felt around the bed to wake Billy, but he wasn't there. "Billy!" Areba called out. She was surprised that he did not answer. Areba dragged herself out of bed. "Billy!" She looked around the cabin, then outside the front door. "Billy!" she yelled louder. She went back inside and grabbed her sacred stones. Immediately, she felt a sadness fall upon her. The stones gave her a vision of Billy leaving…forever. With a heavy heart, she fell into a chair and tears flowed down her cheeks. A note on the table caught her eye.

Areba, my darling wife,

I can no longer take food from you and our children so I cannot stay here watching you and the children suffer. One day I hope that you will forgive me for leaving. Love, Billy

With the note in hand, Areba stared at the wall, a numbness in her heart.

Nia knew something was terribly wrong with Areba. Her magic stones told her to go to her older sister quickly. She excused herself from work that day and Foster did not object.

For the first time in all of Areba's years in America, she did not go to work. Mrs. Meaher was concerned and put together a large basket of food, determined to visit Areba. This was the first visit Mrs. Meaher would make to Africa Town. Everyone came to their windows and doors to watch her as she approached Areba's home.

Mrs. Meaher knocked on the door, trying to ignore all the eyes on her. Nia pulled the door open. She was surprised to see a White woman at the door. Mrs. Meaher introduced herself and stepped right inside, paying no mind to the condition of Areba's small home. She immediately went into the bedroom to Areba's side and gave her a hug. Nia prepared the food that Mrs. Meaher had brought and took it into the bedroom. The food gave Areba strength, but her broken heart kept her ill.

It took several weeks for Areba to gain enough strength to return to work. Rumors spread quickly around Africa Town and the Meahers' plantation about Billy leaving, but no one mentioned it around Areba.

CHAPTER FIFTEEN

Several of the residents of Africa Town gathered outside of Kazoola's home discussing how they might be able to cheer Areba's spirits.

"Everyone, please, let Areba go through this time alone. Let's not bother her during her time of grieving," Kazoola advised. "But maybe you're right about spirits needing lifting. Perhaps it is time to celebrate what we do have. We should have a big celebration and invite the American Negroes to celebrate our traditions with music and food.

"Many of us remember that in African culture, all festivals and major events are presided over by a Godmother and a Godfather, which is a position of honor and esteem. I believe that Areba has earned the honor of being the Godmother of this celebration."

The group applauded, and one man spoke up. "We vote for you to be the Godfather, Kazoola, since you've done so much as a leader in our town!" Everyone cheered in agreement.

"Okay, everyone." Kazoola grinned and held up his hands for quiet. "We will need food and lots of activities and for our first festival."

Over the next three weeks, the residents of Africa Town threw themselves into planning the festival. Areba's spirits were lifted as she, too, helped prepare for the celebration. They would celebrate the homeland, their harvest, and give thanks that they were together and free. They called their festival the Homowo Festival. It would become an annual event, held every year in the fall.

When the day of the Homowo Festival finally arrived, Africa Town was alive with music and dancing. Feathers were used on masks and headdresses as a symbol of the ability of humans to rise above problems, pains, heartbreak, and illness.

When they danced they felt reborn and grew spiritually. Tribesmen from various tribes danced together to the beat of different drums. They learned each tribal chant and chanted together, and the Americans joined in. The women laughed and danced together in a circle around a fire dedicated to their rebirth.

Each family brought food from their homes to share. After putting all of the scraps of food together they had a large feast, enough for everyone in attendance.

Meaher witnessed the event from afar. He stood on the outskirts of Africa Town, as inconspicuous as possible so that he did not disturb the great celebration. He was happy to see the Africans enjoy this day together, celebrating their culture. He turned and walked back to his house feeling affection for the Africans because of all they had done for him and his family.

Meaher found himself feeling dizzy and ill. He staggered into his home where Mrs. Meaher quickly assisted him into his bed. Through the night, Meaher became increasingly worse.

The next morning when Areba arrived at the Meahers' home, she found Mrs. Meaher kneeling at her husband's bedside in tears, and a doctor standing by.

"What is wrong with Mr. Meaher?"

"Oh, Areba, he has fallen into a deathly illness and may not recover," Mrs. Meaher said.

The doctor patted Mrs. Meaher's shoulder. "I have done all that I can do. You will need to keep applying cold towels to his body and let's hope for the best." He packed his bag and left the home.

"Areba, please tend to the children and check in on Mr. Meaher throughout the day. I will be here with him," said Mrs. Meaher.

Areba put added effort into care of the children and the home. She brought food to Mrs. Meaher and made sure she had cold towels for Mr. Meaher. That evening, she did not return home. She sent word to Kazoola to care for her children. Areba insisted that Mrs. Meaher get some rest, and she took over, sitting by Mr. Meaher's bed and placing cold cloths on his head and neck to cool him down.

On the second day of the illness, the doctor stepped out of Meaher's bedroom. Mrs. Meaher and all of the servants gathered around to hear the news.

"Mrs. Meaher, may I see you alone please?" the doctor asked quietly. He led her into the room next door.

Areba overheard the doctor tell Mrs. Meaher that her husband was now in a coma. She felt sadness for Mrs. Meaher and her lovely children. As the doctor continued to speak with Mrs. Meaher, Areba turned to share the sad news with the others. The servants looked at one another in disbelief.

She whispered to them, "Some of you may be really happy to see that man die, but you must remember the pain that Mrs. Meaher and the children will feel. They have always been very kind to us. Just remember that, and never gloat over someone's pain. We will all be in his position one day."

Two days later, Captain Timothy Meaher died in his bed. Areba thought that Mrs. Meaher handled his death very gracefully. She had her moments of sadness, but she never shed a tear.

The funeral and burial were held on Meaher's land. Many plantation owners and some former slaves attended the funeral. Nia joined Areba to give her support. Areba and many of the African women prepared a large spread of food to share after the services. There was a mingling of former slave owners, dignitaries, and Mobilians inside the home and out on the lawn. Sadness filled the air.

Ricky looked up from his notebook. "You said that the Africans made their own Africa Town. Is that the same Africa Town where our church is and where our cousins are?"

"The very spot," Papa said with a nod.

"It's strange to think we go to the same church Areba and all those people went to so long ago," Ricky said. "It makes me feel like we're still connected."

"We are, boy. We will always be connected to those who came before us, and to Africa. The people who came to America on the *Clotilda* and were enslaved never lost their identity even though they were taken away from their home in Africa. They never forgot where they came from, and now we won't forget either."

"It's getting late, Papa. I have to go now," Ricky said. He gathered his things and went to get his bike. When Ricky arrived at home he was excited to tell his family what he had learned. His mother and father saw him running across the front yard. In his haste, Ricky tripped on a rock, falling into a huge puddle of mud. His mother started to go after him, but his dad pulled her back.

"He'll be all right. Let him handle this on his own," Cliff said.

Ricky raised his face from the mud and wiped his eyes, his parents could only see the white of his eyes and teeth. Mama placed her hand over her mouth and began to laugh. Daddy joined in the laughter.

"Whatcha laughing about, Daddy?" Ricky stood up, saw that he was covered in mud, and started laughing uncontrollably. "I look like a mud monster, don't I?" Ricky ran to them and rolled himself all over them. The three of them laughed and played together, muddy and wet.

"Come on now, let's get cleaned up," Mama said.

"Mama and Daddy, I have so much to tell you about what I learned from Papa."

"Just put it all in your report, and we will read it," Mama assured him.

"But..."

"But nothing, boy," his Daddy said. "Get cleaned up so we can go get some dinner and then you need to go to bed."

The next morning Ricky rushed back to Papa's house. He was eager to hear what happened next.

After Meaher's funeral, Nia and Areba walked through the brisk night air hand-in-hand.

"Life seems to be so short," Nia said.

"I know...I am just glad that you and I are able to spend this time together before our end of time," Areba said.

"Me too. I would have been so lonely here without you. I miss Mama and Papa and our family so much." Nia sighed. "What happened to our plans to go back home, Areba?"

"So much has happened, Nia." Areba paused for a moment. "You may be returning to Africa sooner than you expect."

"What do you mean?"

"Dear sister, I have something to tell you, but you must promise not to be sad. I've been very sick. The doctor told me he is doing everything he can to make me better, but the medicine is not working."

Nia placed her arm around Areba and held her tightly. "Oh sister, what can I do? Can the sacred stones help?"

"The stones have not helped me. If God wants me, there is nothing that the stones can do," said Areba.

"I will always be here for you, Areba," Nia promised.

Areba held Nia's hand tighter and looked at her in the moonlight. "Nia, listen to me. I have prepared for when my time comes. I have several people that I trust to take care of my children. I do not want you to be burdened with them because you have another calling. Your place is in Yoruba… leading our people."

"What do you mean…leading our people?"

"Sweet sister, you must remember the day that I found the sacred stones and Mama told us that whoever possessed the stones would be a leader of our people."

"I do remember," said Nia. "But we have led our people here, in Africa Town. Surely we have done what we were meant to do."

"There is more in store for you, Nia. When I held the sacred stones and prayed for you to be safe after I go to the heavens, I saw you in Yoruba leading our people. I don't know when it will happen or how you will get there, but it will happen."

Early one Sunday morning, Nia was awakened by the sound of horses and a wagon rolling into the yard. She peeked out of her window and saw Captain Foster holding the reins of his two new and unruly horses. Wondering where the driver was, she rolled out of bed and put on her robe.

Downstairs, she stepped through the back door of the kitchen. Foster was trying unsuccessfully to maneuver the horses and wagon.

"Good morning, Nia," Foster called. He took one step down from the tall seat. Suddenly, something spooked the horses and they reared up, sending Foster through the air.

Nia's stomach dropped at the sound his body made when it hit the ground, and she ran to him. "Foster! Are you all right?" She crouched next to him and saw that his eyes were closed and blood slowly oozed from the back of his head. "Captain Foster!" She put her ear to his chest and was relieved to hear his heart still beating. "Thank God!" She tore a long piece of cloth from her dress and gently wrapped it around his head and placed it on the grass. "You'll be all right, Captain Foster. I will run to the road to get help."

Foster was badly injured. For several days Nia sat at his bedside as he lay unconscious. His body was filled with fever. On the seventh day, Nia was bringing a tray of tea to his room when she heard his voice from within.

"Nia! Nia!"

She hurried up the remainder of the stairs to his room and when she pushed the door open, she saw his eyes open for the first time since the accident.

"What happened?" he asked weakly.

Nia set down the tray and sat in the chair next to his bed. "You had an accident with the horses and wagon, sir. You have been unconscious for seven days. The doctor has been here every day, sir." She looked down at her lap. "He said that you are suffering from a concussion that enlarged your brain, and..."

"Just tell me, Nia...what did he say?" he asked.

Her face crumpled. "He said that the swelling won't

stop and you may not have long, sir." Her head dropped onto his chest and tears soaked his shirt. "I am so sorry," Nia whispered.

"Nia, please don't cry," he said, touching her head lightly. "I want you to know something. I promised you long ago that I would always take care of you. If I do not recover, I want you to see my lawyer, John Johnston. He will tell you all you need to know."

Nia watched him drift to sleep. She wondered what would happen to her if Foster died. *Where will I go? What will I do?*

Nia finally fell into a worried sleep in the rocking chair. She did not see Foster wake up and open his eyes. He looked at Nia and a smile crossed his lips. Then he settled his head into the pillow and fell asleep once more.

The next morning Nia woke to bright sun shining through the curtains. She stood and stretched and immediately looked to Foster. He lay there, too still.

"Captain Foster," she said, putting a hand on his shoulder. "Captain Foster!" There was no answer. She shook him frantically. "Captain Foster, oh God, no! Please! Foster!" she sobbed. Nia bent over him, weeping into his neck. She felt no warmth from his body and knew he was gone.

After Nia notified the authorities, she went to Areba's house. When she drew near, she saw Areba standing outside of her home waiting to console her sister.

"You already know, don't you, sister?"

Areba held Nia and replied, "Yes. The stones showed me Foster and I knew you would come." Areba took Nia's hand and sat down with her on the front steps.

"You look very weak sister," Nia said, concern in her voice. "What is wrong, Areba?"

"I want to share something with you, Nia." Nia waited expectantly. "I know that this is a hard time for you and this may not be a good time to tell you, but I have always been honest with you. I am not too far behind Foster." Nia shook her head, but Areba continued with a gentle firmness. "It is time for you to take my stones and combine them with yours. You will be taking them to our homeland soon. They will help guide you as you build up the village."

Nia looked at Areba with shock and worry. "How am I supposed to do that?"

"You will find the way very soon. The sacred stones will pave the way for you." Areba held her sister's gaze. "You are the one, Nia. You will be a great leader, and one day you will be able to change the lives of our people."

Nia placed her hand on Areba's mouth. "I don't want to hear that foolishness, Areba. I'm not going anywhere without you. You cannot leave me alone. You just can't—you're all that I have." Nia started to cry.

"That is where you are wrong, my loving sister. I will never leave you in this life or the next. Wherever you are, I will be there also. In life and death, we will always be together," Areba promised. The sisters embraced and their tears flowed freely.

"I have prepared my children as well," Areba continued when they had dried their eyes. "They know that they will see you again some day and that you are going home to help our people. They have strong relationships with those who will care for them when I have passed on."

Areba drew a small bundle from the pocket of her skirt. She opened Nia's hand, pressed the stones into her palm, and closed her fingers around them, holding Nia's hand in both of her own.

"How will I know what to do?" Nia asked.

"Don't worry. Everything will fall into place. Just go back to your home at Foster's and the stones will guide you." They rose from the steps and embraced once more.

"I will look in on you every day," Nia promised. She backed away, still looking at Areba and then turned to walk away. She walked slowly, nearly returning to her sister, but finally made her way out of Africa Town. As she walked she thought about her sister's words and tried to imagine herself as a Yoruba leader.

CHAPTER SIXTEEN

Grief-stricken and afraid, Nia stayed up all night thinking about what she was going to do. Her sister was dying, her master was dead, and she had no home, no money, and nowhere to go. Finally, she drifted into a light sleep in the early hours of morning.

The next morning, a strange man in a suit visited the Foster plantation. Nia answered the door reluctantly, wondering if the man was going to ask her to leave her home.

"I am John Johnston, Mr. Foster's lawyer," he announced. "Is there a Ms. Nia here?"

"Yes sir, would you like to come in?" Nia asked.

She led him to the study where Foster held his meetings. "Just a moment and I'll bring some tea," she said, thinking of Captain Foster's promise that this man would tell her what she needed to know.

Nia returned shortly with the tea and served her guest. She sat down across from him and he asked again, "Is Ms. Nia here?"

"Yes sir, I am here. I am Nia."

He dropped his teacup and a dark stain spread across the rug. "You? You are Nia?"

"Yes, sir," Nia replied.

Mr. Johnston stood and crossed the room to look out the window before pacing back and forth. "Well, I never… How could a nigger?" Finally, he stopped in front of Nia, scowling. "Ma'am… Mr. Foster left it all to you. Everything! His money, land, and assets are worth five hundred thousand dollars," he said angrily.

Nia stood. With a calm voice she responded, "I see. Is there anything else?"

He looked at her, startled. "Well." He pulled a stack of papers from his satchel. "You need to read and sign these. You can read, can't you?"

"Yes, sir, I can."

"Never mind about that anyway," he said, suddenly in a rush. "Just sign your name here." He handed her the set of papers, pointing to the line awaiting her signature.

Nia accepted them and sat down at Foster's desk. The lawyer sputtered and she hid her smile. Nia proceeded to read every line. After she was satisfied that this was no trick or lie, she signed her name.

"Is that everything?" she asked.

"That is everything, young lady. You can now go to the bank and collect your funds and the title for the property," he said.

"Thank you, sir." She stood and ushered him to the door. He nodded once and left. She closed the door and leaned against it, smiling and holding the papers to her heart. "Areba was right," she whispered. "The stones are looking out for me. And Mr. Foster," she added, looking up, "you really did care for me. Thank you."

She heard a knock on the door and figured it would be the lawyer again. She pulled the door opened asking, "Did you forget something?"

Nia sucked in her breath. Her niece Minnie, Areba's oldest daughter, stood there with tears running down her face.

"Auntie Nia, it's Mama. She made me promise to tell you that she was on her way to heaven and that I should say it with a smile, but I can't, Auntie Nia," she cried, falling into Nia's arms.

"Oh, Minnie. Stay right here. I will get my overcoat and go there with you," Nia said, trying to be strong.

"They already took her away, Auntie Nia." Minnie wiped her eyes.

Nia closed her eyes and sagged against the doorframe. "She's gone?" Minnie nodded. Nia stood still for a moment with a heavy heart looking past Minnie staring into the distance. She slowly gazed down at her niece and as tears rolled down her cheeks, she realized that she needed to momentarily put her own sorrow away. "Come in, child. We'll have some tea." They put their arms around each other, holding each other up as they walked into the study. Nia set the legal papers down on Foster's desk.

When they had settled in next to each other on the sofa, Nia turned to her niece. "Tell me about it," she said sadly.

"You know she's been sick. We all knew she would go soon." Minnie took a shaky breath and her eyes filled. "This morning, she just didn't wake up." Nia squeezed

Minnie's hand. "She'd been telling us to be strong. And she told me something to tell you, too. Mama said, you need to remember what she told you," Minnie said carefully, wanting to get it right. "The funeral is tomorrow—you'll have a chance to say good-bye then."

Nia nodded. "What can I do? Are the other children all right?"

"My sisters and brothers will be taken care of by very kind neighbors. They have been good to us while Mama's been sick. I will be going to stay with Mr. Kazoola and his wife." Minnie paused. "Nicky asked how come you can't take care of us, and Mama said you are going to Africa. Is that true?"

"Yes," Nia said, her heart aching at the pain on her niece's face. "I have to go back and help our tribe. You were born here in America, but Africa will always be my home. I hope some day you will get to see it."

"Mama told us that one day you would come back."

"Yes, sweetie. I will come back to see all of you. I promise."

"I will be waiting," her niece said with sadness.

They stood and hugged tightly. Nia walked Minnie to the door and bid her good-bye. "I will see her tomorrow then," she added softly.

The next day Nia stood at Areba's grave. The service was beautiful. Everyone in Africa Town had came to celebrate Areba. Kazoola spoke, and Areba's children laid flowers on the dark and fragrant earth. Mrs. Meaher and her children came, too. Mrs. Meaher smiled when she saw that Areba would be buried in the dress she had given her. She stood and stared, tears flowing down her cheeks. She realized that she hadn't even cried when her own husband died. It was that moment that she realized just how much Areba meant to her.

Nia's tears continued to flow for a long time after everyone had left. She stayed there, talking to Areba and remembering everything her sister had told her. When she finally turned from the grave, Nia had gained a new strength and lost all fear of the unknown.

Later that evening, she returned to Foster's plantation and gathered all the workers together outside the home.

"My Brothers and Sisters," she began, "I'm sure some of you have already heard. Captain Foster has died. "The people looked at each other and spoke in low voices. Nia continued, "He was a horrible man to take us from our land, beat us, and make us work without pay. However, over the years I saw a change in Captain Foster. He had a heart in that body. In his dying breath he told me that he would always take care of me. I confess I did not believe him until after his death. He has left his plantation to me!" Everyone looked at her in amazement and their murmurs grew louder.

"You all have slaved here and made this place what it is today." Nia took a deep breath. "Because of your hard work, I am leaving the property to each of you."

The group erupted, some in exclamations of joy, others in disbelief.

Nia held up her hands for quiet. "I am going back to Africa, where I will help our people," she announced. "For those who wish to come with me, the journey will be long and difficult. We made it once, against our will, and now we will make it again, by choice. Whatever you decide, may you all live prosperous lives in freedom with your loved ones." They all cheered and hugged one another while Nia looked on, smiling.

Ricky and Papa were sitting at the table having a piece of blackberry pie for dessert. "That's it," Papa said.

Ricky put down his fork. "That's it? What do you mean? What happened to Nia and the sacred stones? Did she make it back to Africa?"

"So the story goes."

"But don't you know? I mean, you married Minnie! And Nia promised Minnie that she would come back. Did she?"

Papa took a bite of pie. "I didn't meet Minnie until years later, boy, when she was all grown up."

"But she must have told you!"

Papa pushed away his empty plate. "I'm tellin' you, Ricky, that's all I know of the story. You got plenty to write for your school essay."

At home, Ricky pulled out his notebook, now full of his family's story, and painstakingly began writing his essay.

On the day the class was to receive their graded papers, Ms. Jones called Ricky to the front of the room.

"Ricky, I called you up here because I have something really special for you. Class, you were asked to write about the history of Mobile for your report. Ricky chose to write about a slave ship that came to Mobile called the *Clotilda*. I read Ricky's report and I would like to share two things with you. One, Ricky received an A+ on his report." She began to applaud and the class followed her lead.

"The second thing is quite a surprise. Mobile has some really special visitors coming to town tomorrow. In Ricky's report, he wrote about an African tribe called the Dahomey who kidnapped members of other tribes and sold them to American White men as slaves. Some of those slaves were brought to Mobile on the *Clotilda*. It was a big surprise to learn that one of the women who was on the *Clotilda* is Ricky's ancestor.

"The descendants of the Dahomey tribe are very sorry that their ancestors kidnapped fellow Africans, so they decided to come to America to apologize to the ancestors of enslaved Africans. They are scheduled to come right here to Africa Town in Mobile tomorrow. The big surprise is that Ricky and his family have been invited as special guests to go to the ceremony."

The entire class stood and applauded while Rick stood wide-eyed with his mouth open from disbelief and surprise.

CHAPTER SEVENTEEN

On the day of the ceremony, a delegation from the Republic of Dahomey, which included Tahirou Coutoucou, Dahomey's Ambassador to the United States, came to Mobile and met with the people of Africa Town and dignitaries from Mobile and Washington, DC, at Union Baptist Church.

Mobile's mayor, Joseph Langan welcomed everyone and thanked them for coming. "This is a historic day for Mobile and for the nation as well," he said. He then introduced John Andrews, the democratic senator from the state of Alabama.

Senator Andrews thanked the mayor and turned to the crowd. "I am here as a representative of the United States Congress," he began. "I want to apologize to African Americans on behalf of the government of the United States for the wrongs committed against them." He also apologized to their ancestors who suffered under slavery and the Jim Crow laws that for years discriminated against Blacks as second-class citizens in American society.

He continued, "You have known many hardships, but

you have demonstrated your resilience in the face of so many challenges. Today, we are asking for your forgiveness."

Ricky sat and listened attentively, but could not understand all the words the senator used. Nevertheless, he, like so many others sat patiently waiting for the speaker from Africa.

The senator apologized to all descendants of slaves for slavery ever existing. He also apologized to all the descendants of slave owners for having to bear the fact that someone in their family had owned a slave.

Finally, he asked all Americans to remember the past, and to make sure it never repeated itself in this country. The crowd applauded with enthusiasm.

Next, Mayor Langan thanked Senator Andrews and introduced Ambassador Coutoucou from the Republic of Dahomey.

Dressed in traditional African clothing, Ambassador Coutoucou rose to shake hands with and embrace Mayor Langan.

Suddenly, the door of the church burst open. The crowd's attention was diverted to a man walking up the aisle of the church. Ricky turned in his seat to see what everyone was looking at. When he saw who it was, he nudged Papa and they both turned to see old man Scott. His eyes met Papa's and the two men stared at one another until he found a seat.

The ambassador began to speak. Ricky listened with anticipation. He noticed that everyone in the crowd seemed as eager as he was to hear what the ambassador had to say.

"Good afternoon, my brothers and sisters. The president of the Republic of Dahomey and the people of Dahomey have asked me to come here to apologize on behalf of our government, for the Dahomey people, and for Africa, for the horrible acts that our ancestors committed against their own people. There is no doubt that we are still haunted by our past. Senator Andrews, our people share part of the blame for what happened centuries ago.

"I must own, to the shame of my own countrymen, that your ancestors were kidnapped and betrayed by those of your own complexion, who were the first cause of your ancestors' exile and slavery. But if there had been no buyers, there would have been no sellers. By the same token, if there had been no sellers, there would have been no buyers. Our journey was not to find fault in the buyers or sellers, but to sincerely apologize for the inhumane and tragic events that caused you to be here today. Our ancestors, who caused so much pain, should be standing here looking into your eyes and seeing your pain. But they cannot be here. I can, and that is why I am here today." His voice cracked as tears rolled down his face and he wiped the tears with a handkerchief.

His tears at three separate times during his speech were convincing enough to show that he was sincerely sorry, Ricky thought.

Ricky looked at Papa and saw that he was crying, too. One of Papa's tears fell onto the program he was holding. Ricky looked around the room and saw that almost everyone was crying. Mr. Coutoucou continued.

"My generation cannot begin to imagine what would

cause such a horrible injustice; however, we have learned from our ancestors' mistakes. We have learned that our brothers and sisters are all creatures from God's own image and desire to be treated with the love and care of a new born infant. We want you to know that we are here to give you that love. Slavery was an atrocity, committed from the depths of the darkest parts of the human soul. Africans were captured during tribal wars and seized from their villages, and sold into lives of servitude in a foreign land. It is time to face our past and reach out."

Filled with emotion, the ambassador raised his voice and completed his speech. "We are reaching out our hands to you to let you know that whenever you want to come home, we will welcome you with open arms. The Dahomey Family sends you their love. Thank you."

The crowd stood and filled the church with intense applause. The ceremony continued as they walked to the Africa Town cemetery to lay a wreath at the entrance of the gravesites of all of the former slaves. When they arrived at the cemetery the minister from the Union Baptist Church asked everyone to bow their heads as he said a prayer.

"Whether fault lies with the Africans who sold their own kind to foreigners, with the Europeans who took the international slave trade to the New World, or with all those who owned slaves, there is a great deal of blame to go around for the centuries during which Africa was drained of her people. Many of us here today have blood ties to Africa, and despite the reality of what happened there almost four hundred years ago, it is our hope and prayer that Africans and African-Americans will know that we are one. We have common ancestry and we will always be intertwined. If we refuse to acknowledge all who are guilty in the trans-Atlantic slave trade, we know that we create a false history.

"Even though we here today are not responsible for the sins of our ancestors, we know, Lord, that there is healing in repentance and forgiveness. For even the crimes of our ancestors affect the lives of our children's children. Those who repent of wrongs done, and those who forgive those wrongs, will find your peace, and that may change the course of our nations."

After the prayer, the African delegation paid their respects to the ancestors with libations and prayers. A moment of silence ended the ceremony.

After the ceremony, Ricky ran to the ambassador of Dahomey and introduced himself. "Hello, Ambassador. My name is Ricky. I liked your speech today."

"It is a pleasure to meet you, Ricky," he said while holding out his hand to shake hands with Ricky. Cliff and Papa watched the ambassador smile as he spoke to Ricky.

"I am really glad that you apologized today," said Ricky. Cliff bumped Ricky in the back to keep him quiet.

"Oh? And why is that, Ricky?" the ambassador asked.

"Because those slaves were my ancestors. Papa here told me all about how they were treated by your ancestors. I'm not mad or anything like that, but it was a nice thing for you to do."

The ambassador looked at Cliff and Papa with sadness in his eyes. Unexpectedly, he bent down right in front of Ricky.

"Ricky, I know that my ancestors really hurt your ancestors and they were wrong. My heart truly hurts because of what happened to your ancestors. With all my heart, I ask that you forgive them and all of my people that had anything to do with those heinous acts. Would you please forgive us?"

Ricky paused and looked up at Cliff and Papa. "I wouldn't be Cliff's son if I didn't forgive, sir. As my daddy and Papa have always told me, we all make mistakes and only those without sin should cast stones. That means that no stones should be thrown at all because we have all sinned. Right, Papa?"

"That's right," Papa said with a big smile. "I couldn't have said that better from the pulpit."

Ricky turned to the ambassador. "Yes, Ambassador, I forgive you," he said, leaning in to give him a hug.

"You have raised a good son sir," the ambassador said shaking Cliff's hand. The ambassador bid them good-bye and they watched him walk away.

The trio turned and saw old man Scott walking toward them.

"Oh no, what now?" Papa said under his breath. When old man Scott reached them, he looked at Papa and held his hand out without saying a word. Papa paused for a moment and then slowly raised his hand and put it in Scott's. Their eyes spoke volumes though they remained silent. Something akin to a smile crossed their faces and they released each other's hands. Ricky looked up at both of them in amazement.

Papa walked away with a smile and spring in his step as if he had won a prize.

"Papa and Ricky, would you like to go fishing?" Cliff asked.

"Oh yes! Can we go to our favorite spot? I want to see the *Clotilda* again. Maybe I will get inspired to write part two to my story!" They all laughed.

As soon as the three of them arrived at the bay, Ricky grabbed his pole and quickly ran down to the *Clotilda* while Cliff and Papa got settled on the shoreline. Ricky dropped his pole, only wanting to examine the pieces of the *Clotilda*'s hull. He held onto a piece of the wreck and looked across the bay to the ocean, thinking about his ancestors and all that they had gone through on this ship. He could not believe that after one hundred years, he had the opportunity to touch this old burned-out ship, and now it was almost gone, disintegrated, washed away by years of tropical storms, hurricanes, changing currents, and shifting sands.

Something caught his eye. In between two planks in the murky water was something shiny. He reached down, pushing himself to reach down further. Finally, his fingers closed around a shiny rock covered with mud and seaweed. He cleaned the rock in the water. He stared at it for a moment, thinking. He tried to dismiss his thoughts, but he couldn't stop thinking about the story of the magic stones. Could it be the one Areba lost on the ship?

"Ricky! Come on over let's get started," Cliff yelled. Ricky put the shiny stone in his pocket and ran to meet his father and Papa.

The three of them sat together, fish lines thrown out into the bay.

From Historic Sketches of the South, Emma Langdon Roche, Published in 1914 – The burned out hull of the *Cloltilda.*

Timothy Meaher organized the last slave shipment to the U.S. In 1860, an illegal endeavor since January 1, 1808. Courtesy of Erik Overbey Collection, The Doy Leale McCall Rare Book and Manuscript Library, University of South Alabama.

Cudjo"Kazoola" Lewis (ca. 1841-1935) was a founder of African Town (now Africa town) and was the last survivor of the *Clotilda*, the last ship to illegally transport captive Africans to the United States. Courtesy of Erik Overbey Collection, The Doy Leale McCall Rare Book and Manuscript Library, University of South Alabama.

Phillip "Papa" Robinson

USS Constellation: The *Constellation* served in the Mediterranean Squadron from 1855-1858 and was used primarily for diplomatic duties. She was flagship of the USN African Squadron from 1859-1861. In this period she disrupted the African slave trade by intercepting three slave ships and releasing the imprisoned Africans. During the Civil War, the *Constellation* sailed the Mediterranean to deter Confederate commerce raiders, cruisers, and blockade runners. Photograph taken in Baltimore, Md. by Rick Richardson (2009).

The Civil War was the deadliest war in American history, with over 675,000 soldier and civilian casualties. The war ended slavery in the United States, restored the Union by settling the issues of nullification and secession, and strengthened the role of the federal government.
Photo taken in Washington D.C.
Photograph by Rick Richardson (2009).

Africa Town houses in Mobile, Ala.
Photograph by Rick Richardson (1992).

Union Baptist Church in Africa Town.
Photograph by Rick Richardson (1992).

Africa Town Cemetery. A large number of the *Clotilda's* descendants are buried here. The headstones face Mobile Bay, as if gazing toward the *Clotilda*—the ship that brought them so many miles from their homeland to America.
Photograph by Rick Richardson (1992).

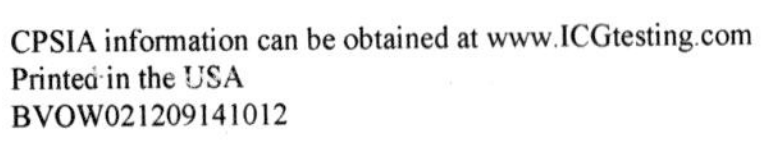
CPSIA information can be obtained at www.ICGtesting.com
Printed in the USA
BVOW021209141012

302893BV00005B/4/P